CW00822844

James Philip

Operation Anadyr

TIMELINE 10/27/62 - BOOK ONE

Cover Artwork concept by James Philip
Graphic Design by Beastleigh Web Design

———

The Timeline 10/27/62 Series

Main Series
Book 1: Operation Anadyr
Book 2: Love is Strange
Book 3: The Pillars of Hercules
Book 4: Red Dawn
Book 5: The Burning Time
Book 6: Tales of Brave Ulysses
Book 7: A Line in the Sand
Book 8: The Mountains of the Moon
Book 9: All Along the Watchtower
Book 10: Crow on the Cradle
Book 11: 1966 & All That
Book 12: Only in America
Book 13: Warsaw Concerto
Book 14: Eight Miles High

Coming in 2020

Book 15: Won't Get Fooled Again
Book 16: Armadas

Standalone Timeline 10/27/62 Novel
Football in The Ruins – The World Cup of 1966

Timeline 10/27/62 Stories

The House on Haight Street

**For all the latest news check out
www.thetimelinesaga.com**

"It shall be the policy of this Nation to regard any nuclear missile launched from Cuba against any nation in the Western Hemisphere as an attack by the Soviet Union on the United States, requiring a full retaliatory response upon the Soviet Union."

John Fitzgerald Kennedy, President of the Unites States of America
22nd October 1962

"Should war indeed break out, it would not be in our power to contain or stop it, for such is the logic of war. I have taken part in two wars, and I know that war ends only when it has rolled through cities and villages, sowing death and destruction everywhere."

Nikita Sergeyevich Khrushchev, Chairman of the Council of Ministers
of the Union of Soviet Socialist Republics
26th October 1962

"We're going to blast them now! We will die, but we will sink them all! We will not disgrace our Navy!"

Valentin Grigorievitch Savitsky, Captain of Project 641 Class Submarine B-59
27th October 1962

Chapter 1

An extract from 'The Anatomy of Armageddon: America, Cuba, the USSR and the Global Disaster of October 1962' reproduced by the kind permission of the New Memorial University of California, Los Angeles Press published on 27th October 2012 in memoriam of the fallen.

The B-59 was less than two years old when her commander, Captain Valentin Grigorievitch Savitsky, conned the diesel-electric submarine out into the cold waters of the Kola Inlet to depart from Murmansk the home port of Northern Fleet for the last time on the first day of October 1962.

Sailing under sealed orders that were only to be opened after the B-59 reached the open sea neither Captain Savitsky nor his crew of seventy officers and men could have guessed that within days their vessel was destined to become the trip wire at the leading edge of the most reckless – and possibly the most ill-considered - act of international brinkmanship in history.

The B-59 was the flagship of a flotilla of four Project 641 submarines – the others being the B-4, B-36 and B-130 – dispatched from their icy Arctic bases on the Kola Peninsula to the warm waters of the Caribbean to participate in *Operation Anadyr*, the mission to deliver medium range ballistic missiles and to set up a

7 | P a g e

permanent Soviet military presence on the island of Cuba. Each Project 641 (designated *Foxtrot* by NATO) Class vessel was equipped with ten torpedo tubes and armed with twenty-two torpedoes, of which one was nuclear-tipped with a warhead generating an explosive potential approximately equivalent to that of the bomb dropped on Hiroshima.

Back in May 1962 the Soviet high command dreamed of establishing a major *blue water* naval base at Mariel, some forty kilometres west of Havana. The initial plan had been to station cruisers, destroyers, several support and repair tenders, and a large squadron of diesel-electric submarines – including seven Golf (Project 629) submarines armed with SSN4 medium range ballistic missiles – opposite the Gulf coast of the USA. However, by the time the B-59 nosed out into the White Sea at the beginning of October, the grand plans for Mariel had been quietly scaled down and only the four Foxtrot class boats were actually dispatched. However, even this reduced Soviet *gesture* – four newly built but old-fashioned, essentially updated versions of German U-boat designs captured in 1945 – set deafeningly loud alarm bells ringing across the other side of the Atlantic.

In October 1962 the United States possessed the biggest navy in the world. Although many of its units were modernised World War II vintage hulls, the USN stood astride the oceans of the globe unchallenged in ways the British Royal Navy, even its halcyon years in the late 19th Century might have envied. Each of its big fleet carriers carried scores of strike aircraft and up to forty nuclear warheads in its magazines. The US submarine service had stolen a giant march on the rest of the world with its rapidly growing fleet of nuclear-powered attack and Polaris armed ballistic missile boats. In comparison to the United States Navy the Soviet Fleet was obsolete, hardly more than a coastal defence force. Yet, like all great behemoths the USN was strangely insecure in its overwhelming power. While the Soviets gazed on the imperious wall of grey steel that contemptuously blocked their access to the world's oceans, and yearned to get their hands on the glittering prizes of western technological advances that were routinely built into their enemy's battle fleets, they failed to appreciate that their foe's greatest maritime weakness - his Achilles heel - was his own fear and paranoia.

In October 1962 the USN tracked the four Foxtrots from the moment they left port. When it became evident that they had been ordered to approach closer to the East Coast of the United States than any previous Soviet submarines this so alarmed CINCLANT - Commander-in-Chief of Atlantic Fleet - Admiral Robert L. Dennison, that he warned 'it *demonstrates a clear cut*

Soviet intent to position a major offensive threat off our shores.'

Given that the USN had based six George Washington and Ethan Allen Class Polaris-armed ballistic missile submarines at Holy Loch in Scotland – each with sixteen missiles capable of hitting Moscow from British or Norwegian waters – and was about to deploy a seventh vessel with a similar capability, Admiral Dennison's risk assessment bordered on hysteria but such was the mood of the times. Lest it be forgotten, Soviet-US tensions had been ratcheting up, gear by gear for many years by late 1962. The Cuba Crisis was just the latest confrontation in a Cold War that in retrospect had begun with the fall of Berlin in May 1945. Seventeen years later Berlin remained a red-hot potential flashpoint; first there had been a blockade of the city eventually broken by the great airlift of the late forties, now the Soviets had recently cut the city in half with a wall. Then there had been the Korean War, which many in America regarded as a proxy war fought with Chinese blood and Soviet weapons; later the brutal crushing of the Hungarian revolution in 1956 left nobody in the West in any doubt as to the ruthlessness of their enemy. There had been the theft of American nuclear secrets and the Soviets' desperate attempts to match US atomic weapons advances. Barely a year before the Cuban confrontation the Soviets had tested an air-dropped hydrogen super-bomb with an estimated explosive yield of between 50 and 58 megatons of TNT - the so-called *Tsar Bomb* - over the Novaya Zemlya archipelago at Sukhoy Nos. Coming so soon after the Soviets had beaten their American rivals into space it was explicable - for all that it was somewhat surprising - that successive American Presidents had allowed themselves to misinterpret their own strength for weakness.

In the early 1960s paranoia was very much in vogue not just in Washington DC but in many if not all western capitals, including London, Paris, Bonn and Ottawa. That the paranoia was largely misplaced; that it was not generally appreciated that the Soviets were militarily outmatched in every respect barring the number of tanks and conscripts on the ground in Central Europe and knew it, was in retrospect the great tragedy of the age.

Viewed through the long lens of history any balanced, rational, semi-informed assessment of the *actual* strategic balance of forces in late 1962 would have concluded that it was the Soviets alone who had firm grounds for their paranoia.

American and British troops stood ready to meet a Soviet invasion on the northern plains of Germany, American B52s and Royal Air Force V-Bombers stood at the end of runways ready to strike. American Polaris submarines roamed the depths of the northern oceans, Thor ballistic missiles in the United Kingdom and Turkey circled the industrial vitals of western Russia, and almost daily the Americans commissioned a new buried ICBM silo in the mid-west. The West's response to the 'scares' of the late fifties and early sixties had been massive and overwhelming. Mounting Operation Anadyr and in so doing provoking the subsequent Cuban Missiles Crisis was the Kremlin's disastrously miscalculated response to its intense feeling of, for want of a better word, *helplessness,* and in less fevered times, the Kennedy Administration might have understood as much.

Unfortunately, the Kennedy White House was a particularly fertile medium upon which to sow the seeds of Armageddon. The Soviet Union's attempt to place nuclear missiles on neighbouring Cuba came as a shock to a country scarred by previous 'scares'. First there had been the 'bomber scare' of the Eisenhower years, then the 'missile gap', both the poisonous products of abysmal Western intelligence and the vociferous, money-grabbing lobbying of powerful defence contractors. There had never been a time when the USA and its allies had lagged behind the Soviets in either respect. Then the Soviets had put the first man into space. Was nothing sacred? Now there was another 'scare'; the Russians were moving into Cuba. What next? A sudden rain of nuclear fire upon the heartland of the North American Continent? Or perhaps an invasion? In the febrile atmosphere of those times, brazenly sending submarines into waters that the United States Navy – and the entire American body politic – regarded as its own, private sea was in retrospect a provocation of monumentally inept proportions.

Notwithstanding the US Navy's loudly voiced and plaintively expressed *concerns*, the Kennedy Administration initially reacted with a moderation that infuriated CINCLANT, ordering that the four Soviet submarines were <u>not</u> to be attacked. However, the USN was directed to intercept, signal and compel the *Foxtrots* to surface, if necessary, by harassing them with hand grenades and practice depth charges. Aware of the perils involved – even in this compromise with CINCLANT – and to lessen the possibility of an incident the Pentagon sent Moscow a *Submarine Surfacing and Identification Procedures* message, so that the Soviets could inform the captains of the Foxtrots that they were <u>not</u> under lethal attack.

When he was interrogated several months later the Captain of the B-36 denied any knowledge of ever receiving this message. Most contemporary historians now assume that the contents of the USN's communication – if it was ever transmitted, a moot point because the Pentagon has never claimed that the

Kremlin formally acknowledged its receipt - was not passed on to the four Foxtrots by the Soviet High Command.

That this critical message was apparently *lost in translation* is key to comprehending what followed because it transformed what might, in other circumstances have been a tense comedy of errors, into a hemisphere-wide catastrophe. This *oversight*, or perhaps, the Soviet High Command's determination not to be intimidated by the US Navy, was further compounded and confounded on 23rd October. It was on this date that the merchant ships carrying the final consignment of missiles and weaponry to Cuba were *turned around* by Moscow.

Logically, this implied that the four Foxtrots should have been recalled. However, if the evidence of the Captain of the B-36 is to be trusted, it seems that the four *Foxtrots* were *not* notified of this change of plan, *nor* was their mission in any way modified. One is tempted to suspect that the Soviet High Command in the heat of the moment, had forgotten - like a drunken chess player - that they had already placed four hostages to fortune in desperately exposed and isolated positions on the global geopolitical board. In any event after 23rd October the four Foxtrots found themselves in a dire situation.

Remember, although the four submarines were relatively newly constructed, they were essentially old-fashioned World War II era vessels. Their underwater endurance was limited and they were obliged to spend a large amount of time cruising on the surface in order to recharge their electric batteries. Consequently, after three weeks at sea in the North Atlantic their crews were battered and exhausted, the vessels stank with oil and rotting food, sweat and all the other rank bad odours with which submariners of the pre-nuclear propulsion age became of necessity intimately familiar. Not for nothing did the fraternity of submariners, irrespective of political persuasion or allegiance the world over, ruefully refer to their vessels as 'pig boats'. Worse, because the *Foxtrots* had been constantly shadowed and actively harassed by the US Navy every day since leaving Murmansk life on board the submarines had become progressively more miserable, stressful and dangerous. Moreover, although the vessels had been able to eavesdrop on American radio stations during the early parts of their voyages they had received virtually no news from Moscow, and by the third week of Operation Anadyr, they were spending so much time submerged attempting to evade American destroyers that their captains were, effectively, out of contact with the Soviet High Command and in possession of no accurate up to date knowledge of world events.

On Friday 26th October, B-59 was cornered by elements of the USS Randolph's hunting group of eleven destroyers north east of Cuba. Unable to shake off her pursuers and with his electrical batteries nearly exhausted, Captain Valentin Grigorievitch Savitsky took his vessel to the bottom where he waited, while two destroyers directed by the USS Beale, dropped small, hand grenade size practice charges all around him. By Saturday 27th October nobody on board the B-59 had slept for forty-eight hours, the air was fouled and all over the boat systems were breaking down. Suffering from the first stages of carbon monoxide poisoning, frightened, humiliated and desperate, Captain Valentin Grigorievitch Savitsky did exactly what he had been trained to do in time of war. In the circumstances it is easy to understand – but to in no way mitigate – Captain Valentin Grigorievitch Savitsky's actions.

Up on the surface the men of the *USS Beale*, an aging Second World War vintage Fletcher class destroyer recently refitted with state-of-the-art underwater detection sonar and submarine-killing weaponry, had absolutely no inkling that they had driven their quarry too far. Why should they have had any such inkling? They were not at war. They were going about what they construed to be their lawful business in what, basically, they regarded as an American ocean. They had been ordered *not* to attack the trespassing submarine and they assumed their foe knew as much. They were not attacking the grounded *Foxtrot* with guided anti-submarine torpedoes or with patterns of precisely targeted half-ton high explosive depth charges, they were just dropping practice munitions – with puny six-ounce bursting charges incapable of harming a submarine's pressure casing – in the water in her general vicinity. They were not even trying to hit the submerged submarine!

The men on the *USS Beale* had been told that the other three *Foxtrots* had been 'rounded up' without incident and they had every reason to expect – sooner or later – that the B-59 would meekly surface, identify herself and skulk off back to Murmansk with her sisters.

We now know that this did not happen.

We will never know the exact chain of cause and effect that led to Captain Valentin Grigorievitch Savitsky's fateful decision. However, we can reconstruct in general terms what must have happened in those last few minutes.

On the surface the *USS Beale* went about her business, quartering the sea, taking her turn dropping practice charges around the grounded Soviet submarine. Nearby, two of her sisters had locked their sonar arrays on the trapped *Foxtrot*. It was a waiting game. B-59 had no alternative but to surface.

Had the hunters had a sounder grasp of the mentality and the command doctrine of their quarry, they might have adopted a less sanguine and rather more measured approach to the hunt. Unfortunately, neither of these things were well understood at the time by the men in the Pentagon, or in the White House, and nobody in the US Navy was aware that the *Foxtrots* which they had been mercilessly harrying were each armed with a single 13.7 kiloton nuclear-tipped torpedo.

Nor were they aware that Captain Valentin Savitsky was at the end of his tether. B-59's commander was unaware that the other three vessels in his flotilla had already submitted to the US Navy's humiliating *Submarine Surfacing and Identification Procedures* and been allowed to go home. Valentin Savitsky did not know whether war had broken out. Valentin Savitsky, like every man on the B-59 had a blindingly violent headache from breathing the putrid air in the submarine. Valentin Savitsky, his judgement impaired by the onset of carbon dioxide and carbon monoxide poisoning, felt himself to be personally responsible as flotilla commander for the honour of the new Soviet Navy. And Valentin Savitsky needed the consent of only two other men on board B-59 to start a nuclear war.

The names of B-59's Political Officer and of Savitsky's second-in-command are lost to history since Northern Fleet's records were almost entirely lost in the holocaust. However, it is known that Soviet tactical nuclear doctrine held that if all three men agreed unanimously, a nuclear-tipped torpedo might be deployed. Given what happened on the afternoon of Saturday 27th October 1962 it is safe to assume that just such a unanimous decision was reached.

The men in the sonar rooms of the USS Beale and the two other destroyers circling slowly within a thousand yard radius of the B-59 would have detected the outer door of Tube No 1 opening, the explosive rush of compressed air which expelled the torpedo into the grey waters of the Atlantic, and the cavitations of the racing propeller.

On board the *USS Beale* alarms sounded.

Shortly afterwards the warhead detonated under her stern.

Chapter 2

02:45 Hours Zulu
Sunday 28th October 1962
57 Miles ENE of Lowestoft, North Sea

HMS Talavera was shouldering into the south westerly gale blowing up from the English Channel at twelve knots. The destroyer was a long, lean hunter built to be a good sea boat first, second and last but her recently completed reconstruction as a Fast Air Detection Escort had added significant weight topside, and now she rolled without the stiffness of earlier years. Nevertheless, she took the ten-foot seas on her port bow easily enough without the plunging, corkscrewing motion of many of the smaller, older destroyers in the Fleet.

Lieutenant Peter Christopher, who had once been a martyr to sea sickness was immensely grateful for his new ship's relatively sedate sea-keeping characteristics. Especially so, because his duties mostly kept him cooped up in the destroyer's Combat Information Centre beneath the bridge. In heavy weather standing a bridge watch was actually a welcome relief. He was one of the Navy's new breed of Electronic Warfare Officers, a radar and electronics specialist and as such, his posting to Talavera – with her suite of expensive state of the art 'toys', as the Captain called them - had been like all his Christmases coming at once.

Peter Christopher looked younger than his twenty-six years. He was tall, a fraction over six feet, angular rather than slim, with a boyish face topped with tousled fair hair and his grey blue eyes spoke of a keenly intelligent restless mind that was never really truly at rest. In his eight years – after his induction at Dartmouth the first three at University College London studying physics and applied electrical engineering, alternating with detachments to the Marconi Labs in West London and the Telecommunications and the Royal Navy Radar Experimental Establishment at Portland - in the Senior Service he had learned not to transmit his surfeit of nervous energy to the men under his command. He had learned also not to worry about it when he was in the company of friends, or men who'd known him long enough to not treat it as a sign of weakness.

He had been assigned to HMS Talavera half-way through her conversion at Chatham Dockyard. The *Battle class* destroyer had the distinction of having been the last of her class commissioned into the Royal Navy. Laid down late in the Second World War on 29th August 1944 at the yard of Messrs John Brown and Co on Clydebank, she was not been launched until 27th August 1945 and then only to clear the slip. The majority of uncompleted War Emergency Program ships had gone for scrap soon after the war ended but Talavera, after lying half-built, apparently forgotten in a Scottish creek for four years, was taken in hand and eventually commissioned into the Royal Navy on 12th November 1950. In a typical act of Admiralty bureaucratic muddle, she had been mothballed after a single, eighteen-month commission, and but for the decision to convert six aging Battle class destroyers into so-called Fast Air

Detection Escorts, she would probably have been scrapped by now.

So, for all that Talavera had been laid down over eighteen years ago mechanically she was a relatively *young* ship whose youth had been enhanced by the radical nature of her recent conversion. Of the original ship only the hull, engines, funnel, forward superstructure and main armament remained. A huge new lattice foremast had sprouted immediately abaft the bridge - the base of this great structure straddling the entire beam of the ship – topped with a four-ton Type 965 AKE-2 double bedstead aerial. A Type 293Q array was mounted on a platform beneath the huge bedsteads. The Type 965 aerial was the ship's long-range 'eye', the Type 293Q was the most recent derivation of a Second World War vintage gunnery control 'range and height-finder'. Abaft of the funnel all torpedo tubes and light AA armament had been discarded and a big, blocky deckhouse containing generators and radar rooms had been welded to the main deck. Between this new superstructure and the old aft deckhouse, a new lattice mainmast carried a Type 277Q height finder dish and several – variously temperamental - Electronic Warfare Support Measures (ESM) and Direction Finding (DF) aerials. The existing after deckhouse had been extended and strengthened to mount a quadruple GWS 21 Sea Cat surface-to-air-missile (SAM) system. On what remained of the cramped quarterdeck the ship retained its original Squid Anti-Submarine (A/S) mortar.

Peter Christopher had assumed this latter was a design-bureau oversight since given the new profile of the ship with its towering radar masts and a superstructure sprouting with twenty-foot whip aerials, it was hard to see how the Squid could be safely fired over Talavera's bow. Besides, the destroyer's sonar was the one element of her electronic armoury that was distinctly *not* state of the art.

As for the GWS 21 Sea Cat SAM system he was reserving judgement. If the ship was under air attack she would be manoeuvring like a scalded cat and he had no idea how his radars were supposed to lock onto a close range fast moving modern jet aircraft in that scenario. He hoped this was something he would discover during the intensive trials scheduled ahead of the ship's first deployment. The four completed *Battle* Fast Air Detection conversions had all been rotated to the 7th Destroyer Squadron in Malta and he had been wrestling to keep his emotions in check ever since learning of his posting to HMS Talavera.

Thoughts of Malta and the prospect of finally meeting Marija Elizabeth Calleja stirred a welter of perturbing feelings that invariably distracted him from his duties. He had resolved to try to not to think too far ahead, or to take things for granted which might so easily blow up in his face. He did not – for a nanosecond - try to put Marija out of his mind; for that was simply impossible. Instead, he did his best to sit her in a comfortable chair in a side room of his thoughts, somewhere close but just out of his direct line of sight. It was not easy. Just before Talavera had sailed the Captain had taken him aside and confirmed, confidentially, that sometime in March the ship was scheduled to transfer to Mediterranean Fleet. HMS Agincourt was due for a refit and when she returned to home waters, Talavera would take her place at Malta. All things being equal next spring he would finally come face to face with Marija and he hardly dared to believe it.

Life was good.

Peter Christopher refocused his attention on his duties, reminding himself that HMS Talavera's primary role was neither anti-submarine work, nor single-handedly tackling fast jets at close range. The utility of the Squid anti-submarine mortar and the relatively new and unproven capabilities of the GWS 21 Sea Cat System were peripheral to Talavera's primary role. The Navy was planning to build a new generation of big carriers and the converted *Battles*, Agincourt, Aisne, Barossa, Corunna, Oudenarde and Talavera were to act as fast radar pickets in the task groups which would be formed around each of the new ships. In each battle group the big carrier's fighters would deal with air threats; the purpose-built frigates of the carrier's anti-submarine screen would deal with the undersea menace. Of the six *Battle* conversions, four had already joined the Fleet, Talavera was running trials, and Oudenarde was still in dockyard hands at Rosyth, work on her having been delayed two months by persistent labour troubles.

Peter Christopher heard the bulkhead door behind him open, booted feet on the steel deck, then the door being dogged shut again. Nobody in the broad, dimly lit compartment moved or looked around. They had been trying to unpick the mysteries of tuning the foremast Type 965 AKE-2 and the Type 293Q systems in such a way as to eliminate the one interfering with the returns of the other for several days. It transpired that the boffins at Portland had been tinkering with the Type 965 to improve the performance of the single bedstead variant for years but nobody seemed to have considered the ramifications of the most recent modifications for the twin bedstead installations in the last two *Battle* conversions. The first four *Battle* Fast Air Detection conversions had older – unmodified bedsteads – and had not encountered the interference problems Peter and his people had discovered within moments of spooling up the array. They had thought they had the problem cracked twenty-four hours ago but then the wind had started blowing up a Force 8 gale from the south west and they immediately realised they had only half-solved the puzzle.

"Kye, sir," murmured the gruff baritone voice of Leading Seaman Jack Griffin. Griffin was only two or three years his Division Commander's age but he had a lived in, prize fighter's face that added years to him.

"Good man," Peter muttered, accepting the mug of hot cocoa brewed from pure melted dark chocolate, already a middle watch CIC and Radar Room tradition on the newly commissioned destroyer. "What's it like topside?"

"Blowing up nicely, sir," the Leading Rate chuckled. "Every third or fourth wave we're shipping white water over the bow. I reckon we'll empty out a few bunks when we put about."

There were muted guffaws around the compartment.

"You've got an evil sense of humour, Griffin," Chief Petty Officer Max Crawley grunted. He was a small, sinewy man whose head only came up to Peter Christopher's shoulder. He had been in the Navy so long he remembered the last time there'd been a mutiny – at Invergordon, a fortnight after he joined his first ship, the battleship Valiant - and everybody tacitly assumed this would be his last ship. The grizzled CPO had been a tower of strength to Peter in the last few weeks as he struggled to get Talavera's complicated new electronic systems on line. Peter had been appalled, and continued to be appalled, by the slapdash, careless working practices and the poor quality control of much of the work carried out by Chatham Naval Dockyard. Every second weld on the new superstructure had had to be re-welded, cableways routinely breached watertight compartments rather than following prescribed, pre-prepared conduits, every other seal leaked, and whole sections of wiring were missing, or installed in completely the wrong place. To his chagrin he had discovered that nothing on the master conversion planning schematics was to be trusted without exhaustive and time-consuming checks and tests. Peter's division had spent so much time putting right the shoddy workmanship, mistakes and omissions of the dockyard that it was only in the last week, five weeks behind schedule that they had found themselves in a position where they could begin to chase down basic operating faults and start to fully familiarise themselves with their new 'toys'. Without CPO Max Crawley, the nearest thing to a bull terrier he was ever likely to encounter in uniform, Peter knew they would still be tied up alongside at Chatham squabbling with the dockyard's battalion of jobsworths.

Max Crawley was always looking for something with which to knock Jack Griffin down a peg or two. He did not think Lieutenant Christopher was lax when it came to discipline, just a little too one-eyed about the number and variety of complex new gizmos on the converted ship. Crawley was a veteran of the Malta convoys twenty years ago. He had been on a destroyer that had shot itself dry on one run, been forced to dump depth charges over the side to distract charging Italian motor torpedo boats, and attempted to fight off a dozen Stukas with rifles and pistols. But that was twenty years ago, this was now as the old sea salt clung grimly to the back of the EWO's command chair he conceded that HMS Talavera did not like a cross sea any more than any other ship with mostly dry bunkers and empty magazines.

Aye, she would roll like merry hell when they put the helm over, true enough!

Peter Christopher was thinking the same thought as he sipped his steaming Kye. The rich bitterness took his mind off the imperfect circular sweep of the Type 965 repeater in front of the middle-aged radar technician sitting in the chair next to him. Talavera had commissioned with so many niggling problems that there were still nine civilian workers on board; electricians and specialist radar men like Ralph Hobbs, the thirty-nine-year-old Marconi assembly supervisor with whom he had been working for the last two months. Hobbs was bespectacled, six inches shorter than Peter Christopher, balding, and one of those people who lived, ate and drank his work. Having been a wireless operator on Lancasters in the war, he had worked for Marconi ever since his demob from the RAF in 1945. He and the Talavera's Electronic Warfare Officer had quickly formed a strong professional bond, strengthened and nourished by the fact that Peter Christopher was not the kind of Navy man who automatically looked down his nose at people on Civvy Street.

Jack Griffin had brought mugs of Kye for everybody in the CIC, including *the civilian*, as he called Hobbs when the man in question was out of his hearing.

"Thank you, Jack," Ralph Hobbs murmured, not looking up.

"Don't mention it, Chief."

As he spoke *the civilian* frowned hard at the fuzzy green sweep of the antenna through another 360 degrees. The screen seemed to shiver, settling anew several times each orbit and the distortion effect had got worse in the last few minutes. Its other worldly green glow threw the faces of the men around it into cruel reliefs, every deep shadow taking on a sinister hue.

"That's definitely not interference from the Type 293, Peter," the civilian declared, glumly.

"What do you think, Ralph? Something external?"

"It's as if we're sailing across some kind of very strong directional..." The civilian's voice trailed away.

Both men were studying the changing returns on the repeater.

"Are you seeing this, Selvey?" Peter Christopher asked, without turning to look at the specialist manning the range finding Type 293 display.

"Yes, sir. Many low-level contacts climbing..." Leading Electrical Artificer Denis Selvey's voice was distracted as his mind worked through the possibilities. The only time he had seen patterns remotely like the one on the Type 293Q repeater was on a half-forgotten training course over a year ago. That mocked up training display had been a kind of practical joke, a test to discover who was paying attention.

"Are we plotting this?" Peter asked, wondering if he ought to have already ordered somebody to start a tactical plot.

The ship's Combat Information Centre (CIC) was only partially operational because many of the critical automated feeds to the 'plot' - the big table that displayed the tactical situation out to a distance of over a hundred miles - were still nominal, courtesy of the shortcomings of HM Dockyard Chatham.

"No, sir," CPO Crawley reported, standing at Peter Christopher's shoulder. "That's a lot of activity from nowhere in no time at all," the older man observed. The CIC had become deadly quiet. The whir of fans, the hum of the score of cathode ray tubes seemed unnaturally loud. He turned, unbidden. "Griffin, warm up the ops board."

"Aye, aye, Chief." The other man was already obeying as he acknowledged.

Suddenly, there were more contacts on the big Type 965 screen.

The 'ops board' or 'tactical plot' in the CIC was a table on which the outputs of the Type 293 and the Type 965 would automatically repeat providing a foundation of real time tactical data upon which other inputs could be selectively added or removed at a touch of a button to provide a 'layered' representation of the surrounding battle zone. Superficially, HMS Talavera's 'plot' was only a glorified electronic fire control table. However, in a real combat situation it would be continuously updated by additional inputs from other air and sea units and tactical inputs from the flotilla leader or battle group flagship's own CIC. The technical wizardry involved in bringing together and representing, in a coherent and readily translated way the modern three-dimensional electronic battlefield still turned most old Navy men's heads.

"Inform the bridge that the CIC plot is being activated," Peter Christopher called, belatedly taking command of a situation *he* ought to have assumed command of long before Chief Crawley had got the ball rolling.

"Contacts climbing," Called the technician in front of the Type 293 screen. "I'd say at maximum climb rates, sir."

"Bridge acknowledges ops board nominal, sir."

"Thank you." Peter Christopher had never taken his eyes off the screens. "How many is that?" He asked Ralph Hobbs.

"Twenty, thirty. No, no, more than that, a lot more than that..."

Distant contacts were merging together, losing individual identities, coalescing into the unusually noisy electronic background. Automatic systems were attempting to label targets but becoming swamped with real and false returns. HMS Talavera's contact detection and tracking systems were state of the art. It made no difference. Target identification was a mess because *hardly any of the target's transponders were squawking friend or foe codes.* The big Type 965 bedsteads might be all seeing but there simply was not the human or the mechanical computational power to process the mass of returns if the targets were not squawking IFF. Especially, not in an environment in which the atmosphere was buzzing and squealing with a mounting barrage of electro-magnetic countermeasures transmissions. Sooner or later somebody somewhere would work out how to stop the latest radars getting swamped this easily but that was no comfort tonight.

Peter Christopher's mind was racing.

He knew what he was seeing but *he* did not understand it.

However, for the moment the fact that *he* did not understand it did not matter.

He reached for the bridge phone.

"Bridge," rasped the voice at the other end of the line.

"EWO for the officer of the watch, please."

There was a short pause.

"What is it Peter?" Drawled the Talavera's executive office, Lieutenant-Commander Hugo Montgommery.

Peter Christopher had taken a liking to the destroyer's second-in-command from the outset. Hugo Montgommery was an old hand; a reservist who had come back into the Navy after his wife had died – in childbirth – and dedicated himself anew to a career he had previously eschewed for a job in a City of London stockbroker's office and marital bliss on land. Montgommery was calm, patient, very competent and a veritable font of Service knowledge. He was also a good, old-fashioned seaman which was why he had taken the middle watch on this particular filthy North Sea night.

"Are you watching the Type 965 repeater, sir?"

"Yes, looks like it's throwing another tantrum!"

The younger man hesitated for a moment. He glanced at the screen. What it was showing made no sense. None whatsoever. But he did not think the system was throwing a 'tantrum'.

"I don't believe so, sir."

"Oh. Tell me more."

"I think we're watching every single V-Bomber base and every single US airbase flushing their birds as fast as they possibly can, sir." Peter did not recognise his own voice. "Absolutely everything at once, sir."

There was a pause of several seconds.

"Very good. Keep me informed, Peter."

"Jamming," Ralph Hobbs declared, thinking out aloud. "Airborne jamming," he added, as an afterthought. "A lot of it. Many, many frequencies. No, forget that, spectrum-wide jamming!"

Peter Christopher sucked his teeth, glanced around at the other men in the CIC. CPO Crawley shrugged; nobody offered a comment.

"Has anybody ever seen anything like this before?"

There were shakes of the head.

The news about Cuba and America had been worrying but Talavera had been at sea for forty-eight hours, largely out of contact with the outside world barring snatches of news heard in passing. The ship was not at a heightened alert level, although that did not mean a great deal because Talavera was not due to start taking on board the remaining 93 members of her normal peacetime complement of 240 men for another fortnight. Currently, she was operating on a full engineering and sea-keeping establishment, with an over-sized mixed electrical division of specialists and civilian workers. The galley was fully manned but there was nobody to man the guns, the Sea Cat launcher or the Squid A/S mortar, even if *all* the magazines had not been empty. Moreover, many of the sea duty men and engineers on board Talavera were freshly trained recruits straight from shore establishments like HMS Sultan and HMS Collingwood. HMS Talavera was a warship in name alone.

Peter Christopher concentrated on the evidence of the radar screens.

There were a lot of aircraft in the air over East Anglia. Aircraft climbing, fanning out across the North Sea. The jamming was getting worse. He knew that a proportion of the V-Bomber force was often kept on Quick Reaction Alert (QRA) – literally standing at the end of the runway fully fuelled, bombed up and ready to go to war at a five minutes' notice – and that practice scrambles were relatively frequent. But even as he watched the repeater screen more contacts were appearing, climbing like bats out of Hell. *And nobody was broadcasting IFF signals.* Nobody.

"What's going on?"

"Captain in the compartment!" Yelled Jack Griffin.

"As you were," Commander David Penberthy directed evenly.

"The air space over East Anglia is filling up with contacts, sir," Peter Christopher reported. It was vital to report exactly what he was seeing and exactly what he *knew* to be the facts before speculation ran rife.

Commander David Penberthy, the forty-six-year-old captain of HMS Talavera placed a hand on his Electronic Warfare Officer's shoulder for a moment. Like the executive officer, Hugo Montgommery, the Old Man was a World War II veteran, having spent most of the war hunting U-Boats in the North Atlantic. HMS Talavera was the third destroyer he had commanded; a complex, rebuilt ship like Talavera with a largely green crew was invariably placed in a very 'safe pair of hands'.

Talavera's captain was a big man who did not need to raise his voice to be heard or to exert his authority. He was known to have a blowtorch temper and very occasionally, a lashing tongue but from what Peter had seen so far, he was careful to reserve both for people whom he decided were not up to the job.

"What do you think is afoot, Peter?" The older man asked with a conversational sangfroid that left a lasting impression of everybody in the CIC.

Peter Christopher hesitated, collected his wits.

"I'd say the V-Bomber Force has scrambled, sir," he reported, his voice thick with tension.

"I think we have missiles launching!" Ralph Hobbs interjected from out of the nearby, green glowing gloom. "One, two, three..."

Altered symbols danced around the new contacts.

"The ESM and DF arrays are getting swamped with noise, sir," called another voice in the gloom. "All around the compass now, sir."

The Captain of HMS Talavera patted his EWO's shoulder again and stood tall in the eerily illuminated CIC.

"More missiles launching," Ralph Hobbs grunted, not quite believing what he was seeing on the cold, uncaring repeaters.

Commander David Penberthy stepped across to the bulkhead telephone.

"Bridge, this is the Captain speaking." A momentary delay, and then, very calmly, he said: "The ship will come to action stations. Repeat, the ship will come to action stations. I shall be on the bridge directly."

Chapter 3

Lieutenant-Commander   Simon   Collingwood blinked into the harsh light, disorientated for a moment but only for a moment. Then the long conditioning of his eighteen-year naval career kicked into action. He was fully awake even before he rolled onto his side throwing off the sheets and sitting up to peer, irritably up at the silhouetted face of the man standing over his bed in the first-floor room of the dingy hotel fifty yards from the main dockyard gates.

"What's going on?" He asked, not pausing to rub the sleep from his eyes as he planted his feet on the floor and reached for his watch on the rickety bedside table. He became aware that the other man, a very young seaman with a shore patrol band around his right bicep, looked shaken and on the verge of panic.

"War order, sir..."

"What?"

"General war order, sir. It came in a few minutes ago. Your name was at the top of the first emergency duty list, sir..."

Collingwood pushed the seaman aside and groped for his uniform dungarees.

He was a small, prematurely balding, dapper man with a calm, organised mind and a reputation for steadiness in the most stressful of situations.

General War Order! It might be an exercise although deep down he doubted it. Although he had only been paying passing attention to the news lately, and had not read a paper for several days he shared the unease of others in the Mess.

"Who else is on your wake-up list?" He asked brusquely.

"Sir?"

"Never mind. Wake up everybody in this building. All *Dreadnoughts* are to report to the boat *immediately.*"

The man literally ran out of the room.

Nobody at the dockyard gates knew what was going on.

Collingwood flashed his pass and ran between the big, blocky workshops towards the floodlight graving basins in the near distance. Other men were walking fast, several trotting. Nobody gave him a second look.

It was a little surreal. The air was icy cold, the wind spitting sporadic drops of rain. There were no alarms, no klaxons blaring, a few shouted commands in the distance and the sound of running feet, otherwise, nothing.

There were two armed sentries at the main gangway.

Behind them the submarine's tall sail jutted into the night. They had pulled away the cranes and jibs a fortnight ago but multiple umbilicals still snaked from the land down into the carcass of HMS Dreadnought in the dry dock. Power, communications, water. Until the boat's Westinghouse reactor pile was online, she was totally dependent on the land.

There was a fixed telephone link to the Dockyard Supervisor's Office at the head of the gangway.

Collingwood picked it up.

"This is Dreadnought," he reported, breathlessly, "can you tell me what's going on, please."

No, the duty officer could not tell him what was going on.

"The General War Order was broadcast in the clear to all active units and shore establishments at zero-two-three-seven hours Zulu, sir. That's all I know."

Collingwood glanced at his watch.

03:03.

Men were arriving on the dockside.

"Everybody on the boat!" He shouted. "Quickly, now!"

Half of Dreadnought's future crew – including her captain and all bar two of her officers - were hundreds of miles away on the South coast in Southampton training in a specially constructed simulator while the boat continued fitting out at the other end of the country. Dreadnought was not supposed to commission until the spring but to all intents, she was – reactor excepted – practically ready for sea.

Collingwood gazed thoughtfully at the great black whale-like shape of Britain's first nuclear power hunter-killer submarine lying silently, unknowingly in the shadows of the dry dock beneath the blazing floodlights. He had been with the boat eight months overseeing the fitting out. Eighteen years in the Royal Navy, a long, gradual progression from lowly seaman to being posted second-in-command of the most advanced fighting machine in the Fleet. Now war might have been declared and Dreadnought lay helpless in plain sight, like a beached cetacean on the foreshore.

General War Order...

Simon Collingwood tried not the think about the madness those words implied. Not right then. Right then he was thinking that if only the fools could have staved off the insanity for another two, or better still, three or four months, the great enterprise of his professional life would have come to fruition. HMS Dreadnought had been the fulcrum of his existence since long before her keel was laid down on 12th June 1959. For *the boat*; Britain's first nuclear powered submarine to be trapped helplessly in a dry dock in Lancashire when the world might be about to go up in flames was almost unbearable. He had poured so much of his life into the great black hull before him in the dock and now it seemed it might have all been for nothing.

He had been sent to Groton, Connecticut, to train alongside his US Navy 'allies' ahead of joining first the Design Project Team at Barrow-in-Furness, and later being appointed Naval Construction Liaison Officer (Engineering and Electrical Systems) as Dreadnought slowly progressed from a lifeless half-completed hulk to a living, breathing deadly, mind-bogglingly complex fighting machine. Six months ago, he was confirmed as the boat's first executive officer.

General War Order...

The Royal Navy had begun investigating the possibilities of seaborne nuclear propulsion plants as long ago as 1946. The work had never had a very high priority and during the Korean War, in 1952, all research was suspended. It had not been until in 1955, when the US Navy commissioned the *USS Nautilus* that the Royal Navy, until then the acknowledged masters of anti-submarine warfare had awakened to the fact that *everything* had changed. In exercises with the new American vessel it was suddenly horrifyingly obvious that the tactics and the technology that had won the Battle of the Atlantic simply did not work against the new undersea threat. Faced with attempting to join the nuclear submarine building *game* from what was basically a standing start, in the mid-1950s there seemed no prospect of a British version of the *Nautilus* joining the Fleet for at least another decade, or perhaps not even before the end of the 1960s. It was a depressing scenario for the Royal Navy and a shameful one for the politicians who had let it happen by starving the original reactor research project of funds and then compounding their parsimonious blunder, by stopping it dead in its tracks at the very moment the Americans were racing ahead.

Simon Collingwood was one of only a handful of serving officers who knew the whole story of the Royal Navy's race, against all odds, to join the nuclear submarine club. HMS Dreadnought as a project would have been impossible without the transfer of some of the US Navy's most secret and most advanced technologies. Dreadnought incorporated all the lessons learned in the design, construction and operation of the USS Nautilus, enabling the Royal Navy to bypass at least five and probably as many as ten years of horrendously costly development time. That this had been possible at all was down to two remarkable men, and a little-known secret clause in the 1958 US-UK Mutual Defence Agreement.

The first remarkable man was Admiral the Earl of Mountbatten, the First Sea Lord, whom Simon Collingwood considered himself honoured to have been introduced on several occasions. The second remarkable man was Admiral Sir Wilfred Woods, Flag Officer Submarines in the mid-1950s and between 1958 and 1960 Deputy Supreme Allied Commander Atlantic based in Norfolk, Virginia, on whose staff Collingwood had been lucky enough to serve for several months. Mountbatten was the political powerhouse with a trans-Atlantic contact book unrivalled in history; Sir Wilfred Woods was the supremely professional and technically brilliant master submariner who had spent every minute of his time in America making friends.

Initially, the two men planned to build a new generation of *all-British* nuclear boats. Given that the Americans had shut Britain out of the nuclear research loop almost as soon as the Second World War ended, this had seemed the only realistic basis on which to proceed. As late as 1956 Rear Admiral Hyman Rickover, the high priest and implacable guardian of the US naval nuclear power programme had gone so far as to veto Mountbatten's request to visit USS Nautilus. In retrospect this incident proved to be the high water mark of US-British non co-operation in the field because later that year Rickover came to the United Kingdom with a formal offer to supply third generation S3W reactor technology – which was then being deployed in the American Skate class nuclear powered attack boats - to the Royal Navy. Behind the scenes Mountbatten had been hard at work, capitalising on his old friendship with Arleigh Burke, the US Navy's Chief of Operations and subsequently Rickover was persuaded – presumably reluctantly – to agree to the transfer of the *latest* reactor technology under the terms of the 1958 US-UK Mutual Defence Agreement. Thus, HMS Dreadnought was built around an American power plant in a British hull populated with British combat systems, heavily influenced by virtually unrestricted access to the Electric Boat Company's yard at Groton where vessels of the Skipjack class were currently under construction.

General War Order...

Dreadnought was only weeks, possibly days away from 'reactor initiation' and her first scheduled 'in dock' dive trial!

Simon Collingwood stared into the darkness beyond Dreadnought's tall, looming sail to where the first of her 'improved' sisters was already taking shape in an adjacent dock.

The Americans had transferred so much reactor and systems technology and divulged so much operational information that even before Dreadnought had been being laid down, Rolls-Royce, the United Kingdom Atomic Energy Authority and the Admiralty Research Station at Dounreay had begun work on a wholly British nuclear propulsion suite. The first of a new class of nuclear-powered attack boats, HMS Valiant, had been ordered in August 1960 and laid down in January 1962. The partially formed skeleton of the Royal Navy's second nuclear *boat* was invisible in the night on a covered nearby slipway.

More people were collecting on the dockside.

Civilians, men in uniform, milling around, waiting for orders.

"You there!" Collingwood bawled. "You should all be *somewhere*! If you don't know where you are supposed to be report to your ships or take shelter! Now!"

From across the other side of Dreadnought's dock diesel generators were roaring into life. Acrid smoke began to drift to seaward. Thank god somebody's got their heads screwed on, Collingwood thought. He took one last look around and strode up the gangway. He went to the forward hatch, which was unguarded, clambered down the vertical steel ladder into the bowels of the submarine, turned at the foot of the ladder and stepped into the control room.

Collingwood was pleasantly surprised to find more than a dozen men waiting for him. Cables snaked everywhere, through open hatches, coiled on the deck, hanging in tangles from overhead control panels.

"The radio room is manned, sir," reported Lieutenant Richard Manville, the boat's Supply Officer. "The General War Order is being re-broadcast every five minutes in the clear, sir. I've verified its authenticity. This is no drill."

"Very good," Collingwood acknowledged, pleased that the second most senior officer in the compartment was showing no signs of panic. "I have the boat, Mr Manville." He looked around at the faces in the control room. "Until we know what's going on, I want all our people on board." He briefly considered disconnecting the umbilicals and dogging down the fore and aft hatches, decided against it. Theoretically, the boat had viable internal battery power but he had no idea what charge was in the batteries or even if they were fully operable. He stepped through to the radio room. "Do we have a telephone link to the Dockyard Supervisor's Office?"

"Yes, sir."

Then he heard it.

The banshee wail of air raid sirens that he remembered so well from his boyhood in London filtering distantly, eerily down through the open hatches into the equipment-cluttered spaces inside the pressure hull of HMS Dreadnought.

With a horrible, sickening foreboding Simon Collingwood realised that this was indeed no exercise...

Chapter 4

"What is it?" Marija Calleja asked, sleepily.

"I don't know," her mother complained irritably in the gloom.

Marija blinked into a more wakeful state. Why was her mother holding a lighted candle? And what was that noise, that commotion in the distance? Gradually, her ears became a little more attuned to the background clutter. She heard car and truck motors, many, many of them, dozens, perhaps scores of them. There were raised voices in the street outside leading down to the sea, and there was a glare of bright light behind the thick curtains of her bedroom.

"Your father says for us to go down to the cellar," Marija's mother said, growing ever more vexed.

"Papa?"

"Soldiers from the barracks at Tigne woke us up," the older woman explained. "Didn't you hear all the banging! Oh, never mind! You always could sleep through an air raid! Your father went off in the car they sent for him."

"Oh." Marija could hear the rest of the house coming to life. Her second-floor room was at the back of the building on the quiet side of the block with no direct view of either Sliema Creek, or the street outside leading down to the harbour. "What happened to the lights, Mama?"

"I don't know. The power is off. Get up, get up, girl!"

Marija groaned and pushed herself up into a sitting position. She was twenty-six years of age and her mother still called her 'girl'! She let it pass. She loved her Mama dearly and sometimes felt guilty for not being the respectful, obedient, dutiful daughter that her mother still expected her to be, even in this modern world. Mothers, she consoled herself, could not stop being mothers even when their brood was fully fledged and able to fend for themselves. Of course, her Mama had never expected her only daughter to break those shackles in the way her brothers, Samuel, and latterly, Joseph, had broken free in the normal way of all sons. Daughters were different, particularly daughters who had lived the life that she had lived. Marija sighed and began to rouse herself, stiffly from her bed.

In Sliema Creek a ship blew its whistle. The sound reverberated around the house, rattling windows.

Marija shook off her mother's supporting arm.

"I'm getting up. I'm getting up," she protested, rising unsteadily to her feet and shrugging the creases out of her long cotton nightdress. She understood why her mother was still so protective but sometimes it irked her intolerably. She was no longer an invalid and she had not been one for many years. Nor was she a child any more either although she suspected that in her mother's eyes, she would always be twelve years old. Marija would bear the terrible scars of her crippling childhood injuries for the rest of her life but she hated it when she was treated as if she was anything other than fully capable of looking after herself. "Go! Go! Stop fussing over me, Mama!"

Her mother departed huffily.

Marija pulled the curtains aside from her bedroom window. Unable to see anything she went out into the hallway to see what she could see from that vantage point. The Cambridge Barracks astride nearby Tigne Point were a blaze of floodlights, the parade ground and vehicle park dazzlingly illuminated. As she watched a helicopter – a Westland Wessex - swoop in to land in the centre of the open space, and ant-like figures scurry away from it stooping beneath the churning rotors, before the machine lifted into the air and thrummed across Marsamxett to disappear in the night over Valletta.

"Marija!" Her mother called, angrily.

"I'm coming!" She returned to her room and slipped on her sandals, pulled a summer overcoat from her sparsely populated wardrobe over her nightdress and went to the head of the stairs. Her left leg ached but she limped only slightly and the back pains from yesterday – when she had spent almost the whole day on her feet at the hospital – were mercifully absent. "I'm coming!"

She went down the stairs with a confidence that astounded those who had heard her story but who did not actually know her. Her hand rested on the old, warped oaken banister rail but only as an afterthought, just in case she slipped as now and then, happened. Marija Elizabeth Calleja had learned when she was young that life wasn't about how many times one fell over; it was about how quickly one picked oneself up afterwards.

The Calleja family had moved into the old house in Sliema eight years ago. After the war they lived in an apartment in Mdina but when Marija's father had been promoted to Under Manager of what was still, in those days, the Royal Naval Dockyard at Senglea, he had wanted to be closer to both his office and the British headquarters, HMS Phoenicia on Manoel Island. There was some talk at the time of the family moving back to Vittoriosa-Birgu – which would have been right next to the dockyards – but Marija's mother had never been back to the place where in 1941 her brother, sister and her uncle had died, and where she had almost lost her only daughter, Marija.

Marija was about to follow her mother and her youngest brother, Joe, down into the cellar when the strident howl of another ship's steam whistle reverberated across the harbour. On an impulse she ducked out of the front door onto the main street where she had a view straight down the avenue of buildings to a small sliver of Sliema Creek.

When she returned home for the weekend – this month her weekends as defined by the St Catherine's Hospital for Women's nursing rota fell on a Sunday and a Monday - the previous evening there had been four big, grey destroyers at anchor. She had lingered on the waterfront, sat a while on the sea wall and enjoyed the feel of the sun on her face as it set over the lumpy towers of the hospital at Msida, allowing herself the time and the space to think her own thoughts. Her thoughts had drifted, turning slowly around the many good things in her world.

Lately, every time she laid eyes on the ships of the 7th Destroyer Squadron with their ugly, ungainly bedstead radars and their long, gun-bristling hulls she thought about Peter Christopher.

HMS Talavera was a sister to two of the destroyers currently based in Sliema Creek, and inevitably she had begun to dare to wonder if one day, maybe soon, she would be sent to Malta – carrying Peter Christopher - to relieve one or other of her sisters. Of course, she did not – ever – let her thoughts run too far ahead. The immutable lesson of her life was that one had to walk before one tried to run. She knew Peter had had sweethearts in England, and once, one in Simon's Town, in faraway South Africa. She knew also that the life of a career naval officer was hardly compatible with her own, very singular...circumstances. Yet, every time she looked at those beautiful, deadly ships moored in Sliema Creek she allowed herself to dream her dreams. Always a voice in her head told her that those dreams would be her secrets forever; that nothing would ever come of them but that did not matter. She had discovered when she was a girl - imprisoned hopelessly in one hospital bed after another for what had seemed like eternity - that a world without dreams was a world without hope.

Without hope there was nothing.

Marija stared down the arrow-straight street to the darkly glinting waters of the Creek. A tug was dragging the bow of HMS Scorpion off its mooring buoy. She often watched the destroyers slipping their lines, edging out towards the sea. Always, the evolutions were smoothly choreographed, unhurried. Tonight, men were running about the decks in...*panic*. The Scorpion's sharp prow - pointing out into Marsamxett - began to move. A vehicle hooted behind her and she stepped close to the wall of her house as several British soldiers jogged down the hill.

What was going on?

It was a defining characteristic of the British presence - her little brother Joe called it 'the occupation' - on Malta that ships and troops did not *hurry* anywhere. Certainly not in the middle of the night and never ever in the small hours of a Sunday morning. If Malta was in any sense 'occupied' the *occupiers* were as a rule at pains not to overly inconvenience the civil population in any way. Brave little Malta had gone through so much to help the British win the war and memories were long. Marija owed her survival and the fact that she was able to live the life she wanted to a remarkable British Naval Surgeon, without whose intervention she would have lived out her years in a cot, gazing at the world passing her by. Quite apart from her feelings for a certain Englishman – Peter Christopher – whom she had never actually met or spoken to but whose existence indelibly coloured her view of England and the British, notwithstanding the widespread yearning for real Maltese independence, she personally hoped the British would stay forever. If not as rulers then as protectors and friends; firebrands like her foolish little brother might spout all manner of anticolonial rhetoric but most Maltese took a more pragmatic, and yes, sentimental view of these things. So, to see the British running around in what they would call in others 'a dead funk' was more than a little unnerving.

A great gout of steam issued from the funnel of a tug ramming its snout under HMS Scorpion's bow. Marija realised that the destroyer was swinging unnaturally close to the waterfront. With a tingling jolt of icy anxiety, she realised the big ship was so desperate to get out to sea that she must have cut her cables.

What is going on?

Chapter 5

Walter Brenckmann tried to roll deeper into the sheets when the alarm went off seemingly inches from his head. He and his wife, Joanne, had turned in early ahead of their planned pre-daybreak start in the morning. Tomorrow was their twenty-eighth wedding anniversary and Walter had taken several days off so they could drive down to Cape Cod. Joanne groaned, shrugged closer to her husband and for some blessed moments, neither of them was fully awake. Since the kids had moved out – the last, eighteen-year-old Tabatha, just a month ago to head up to New York State where she was boarding with friends of Joanne's sister's family in Buffalo – Walter and Joanne had been struggling to get used to having the big house next to the MIT campus to themselves again. The quietness and the emptiness of the place had spooked them at first, now they had reached the point where they were learning how to enjoy and fully appreciate the peculiar privacy which had returned to their lives for the first time in over a quarter of a century.

They had married in 1934, the year Walter had finished law school at Yale. He had been twenty-five and Joanne had been twenty-eight, a month short of her twenty-ninth birthday. Both families had been quietly scandalised by the age difference which seemed very odd looking back. Joanne had helped pay Walter's way through law school, as a typist nine to five through Monday to Friday, and waiting tables at night. They had started having babies as soon as could be decently arranged. Walter junior had been born nine months and three days after the wedding. Daniel fourteen months later, Samuel within another thirteen months. Tabatha had been an afterthought; an accident many years later. Sam's birth had been *difficult* and the doctors had warned Joanne not to have another baby. *What did doctors know?*

Walter Junior was in the Navy, in the Submarine Service of all things! A lieutenant (senior grade), the Torpedo Officer on the Skipjack class nuclear attack boat the USS Scorpion. Daniel, after various stops and starts had been persuaded to follow in father's footsteps to Yale where he had knuckled down to his studies and was in his last year. Sam, to be different because he was born with a contrary streak a mile wide had dropped out of college, thrown his guitar in the back of his beaten-up Chevy and headed west last year. Sam had inherited his musical itch from Joanne's side of the family. Joanne's uncle Saul had been in Glen Miller's orchestra in the war and made a living playing clubs and bars and halls across the North East ever since. Tabatha had always been closest to Sam but thank God, she retained every ounce of horse sense she had been born with. She had wanted to be a teacher and gone to New York State to study English Literature and Geography. Neither of her parents understood how that combination of subjects worked but what parents ever understood anything about their offspring!

The alarm seemed very *loud*.

Walter Brenckmann rolled onto his back.

22:29.

The screeching, wailing noise was coming from outside, penetrating the battened down bedroom windows.

"Walter?" Joanne groaned. "What's..."

Back in 1940 when Walter and Joanne had realised that - sooner or later - war was coming Walther Brenckmann had put himself forward for Officer Selection to the Navy. If he was going to have to put on a uniform it was *not* going to be that of an infantryman. They had reasoned, his thriving downtown law practice notwithstanding that it would be for the best if he got into the military early. Yes, there had been ways of dodging the draft. And yes, they had explored them, cursorily. But every time they walked through the options; the Navy had recommended itself. Walter's father had been on the battleship the USS Arizona in the Great War and that had worked out well for everybody concerned. He never fired a shot in anger and had come home a hero; nobody in the Navy was going to order Walter to climb over a parapet and walk into a hail of machine gun fire. Hell, nobody was likely to ask him to even personally handle a weapon in the Navy. All the clever money said the Navy would most likely post him straight to the Judge Advocate's Department in the Pentagon. Washington was not that far away, was it? Of course, things had not worked out that way. By the end of the war Walter had ended up in command of a destroyer escort in the North Atlantic and returned home in 1946 with a Lieutenant-Commander's commission in the US Navy Reserve. When the Korean War came along, they had promoted him full Commander and given him a Fletcher class fleet destroyer. So much for the best laid plans...

Suddenly, Walter realised what he was hearing.

The problem was not his hearing, it was his brain.

There were warning sirens every few blocks in metropolitan Boston, fewer in the suburbs and once a year the authorities fired them up with a long-anticipated fanfare. What *never* happened was somebody deciding to wind up the infernal banshee horns at...

He glanced at the alarm clock a foot from his head on the bedside table as the minutes hand clicked onto the half-hour. His ears still did not want to believe the rising pitch of the spine-tingling screech outside the house.

"Basement," Walter croaked, throwing off the sheets. "We've got to get down to the basement, Jo!"

"What are you talking about, Walter?" His wife complained testily, burrowing under the sheets.

"That's the attack alarm," he told her calmly.

"Don't be ridiculous, Walt," she retorted sleepily, sitting up. "I know things are a bit *tense* with the Russians over this Cuba thing, but..."

"It is illegal to sound the alarm without twenty-four hours' notice unless the attack is already under way, Jo!" He snapped, irritably, knowing he was somewhat embellishing the truth. "Bring blankets and grab some warm things. We're going down to the basement until the all clear sounds."

"You really think..."

"I do. I'd rather look stupid than be dead or seriously injured, okay!"

Chapter 6

Commander David Penberthy felt naked on the bridge of HMS Talavera. His feeling of nakedness had nothing to do with the fact his ship was unarmoured, or because his magazines were empty. Even if his magazines had been overflowing with 4.5-inch rounds and Sea Cat surface to air missiles he would have felt just as *naked*. His was the nakedness of a man who knows, with utter certainty, that the world around him has gone mad.

"This is the Captain," he announced, swallowing hard. Painfully aware that he was clasping the microphone so hard his hand was twitching with spasms of cramp he forced himself to relax a fraction. "About half an hour ago CIC became aware of unusually intense unscheduled aerial activity over East Anglia and of what appeared to be a concerted, multi-frequency electronic jamming effort. Fifteen minutes ago, we observed, visually, what appear to be the blooms of two large thermonuclear detonations. The first was on a bearing consistent with an explosion in the vicinity of the Medway Estuary. The second appeared to be in the vicinity of London. We have subsequently observed at least ten further strikes in a wide arc taking in probable V-Bomber and American air and missile bases in East Anglia, all the way south to the capital. We are picking up regular General War Order broadcasts and a large amount of emergency operational communications traffic from Allied forces. Until the situation becomes clearer Talavera will stand out to sea. I know that many of you will be worrying about family and friends ashore," he paused, his mouth dry, "but all we can do for the moment is stand to our stations and do our duty to the best of our abilities. I give you my word that I will pass on any further information I receive as soon as is practically possible. Captain, out."

Penberthy handed the microphone to the Bridge Speaker, an eighteen-year-old seasick boy who had only joined the ship a week ago, one of a draft of fourteen new sea duty men straight from the completion of his thirteen-week basic training at HMS Collingwood in Hampshire.

"Chin up, lad," he murmured, patting the kid's shoulder. "Chin up."

Penberthy had turned Talavera onto a course that would take her out into the middle of the North Sea some twenty minutes before, now she was battering away from the English coast at twenty-seven knots. He felt like a coward, running like a scalded cat with his tail between its legs. He had asked himself what else he could do in the circumstances; no answer had come. Talavera was a warship in name alone. She had her seaworthiness, her radar and her communications suite and that was all. She had no ammunition, nor the trained crews to fight her guns and missile launchers even if her magazines had not been empty. His first responsibility was the safety of his ship and plainly nowhere near land was remotely safe.

"What's the news on our bunkers?" He inquired, grimacing at the ruddy-faced, four-square man who had come onto the bridge as he was addressing the crew.

Lieutenant-Commander John Cook, Talavera's forty-three-year-old Engineering Officer's expression mirrored his Captain's grimace. He had served briefly with his captain many years ago in the Mediterranean on the fast minelayer Manxman. Those had seemed desperate days when the only way to transport vital supplies into Malta - besieged and starving and under constant aerial bombardment - had been to send Manxman and her sister Apollo on forty knot helter skelter night time sorties through the blockade.

"You can have another ninety minutes at these revs, sir," the other man replied, taciturn as ever. As he spoke, he wiped his hands on a rag he produced from his almost, but not quite, pristine uniform boiler suit. "After that we won't have enough fuel to make land," he shrugged, "anywhere."

"Ninety minutes?"

"Aye, sir. That'll run tanks three and four dry, sir."

Penberthy nodded. Talavera had been tasked to be at sea forty-eight hours operating at no more than cruising speed; fifteen to eighteen knots. The galley had taken on seven days rations but the Dockyard Superintendent had allocated a typically miserly fuel reserve despite Penberthy's angry complaints that in her new configuration,

Talavera's centre of gravity would be unnecessarily elevated – making her sea keeping motion worse – for the purpose of running radar trials unless she flooded several of her bunkers. The Dockyard Superintendent did not give a damn whether the reconstructed destroyer rolled like a barge or if her bunkers would have to be cleaned when she got back to port; Penberthy was not going to have a drop more of his precious bunker oil than he absolutely needed.

"What about revs for twenty knots, John?"

"Two hours, maybe." The other man hesitated. "Two-and-a-half, perhaps."

Penberthy contemplated the options. No, he decided, they would continue out to sea at their best speed for as long as they could. As if to emphasise the urgency of putting as much sea room as possible between the ship and the land the enclosed conning bridge briefly filled with blinding light through the aft viewing scuttles.

"Very well. We shall continue at present revs for one hour, Chief."

"Aye, aye, sir." The other man departed back down into the bowels of the destroyer.

Almost immediately, Penberthy was handed another comms handset.

Lieutenant Peter Christopher sounded calm, pragmatic.

"May I have permission to operate at a reduced EWO status, sir?"

"Is there a problem, Peter?" Penberthy asked, his mind still turning over the critical fuel situation.

"I'd like to secure as much kit as possible, sir," the younger officer explained, very patiently. "In case we get too close to one of those *strikes*."

Penberthy's mind clicked back into gear.

Much of Talavera's electronics suite was theoretically, at least, hardened to survive the EMP – electro-magnetic pulse – from the atmospheric detonation of large thermonuclear warheads but this was not the time or the place to be respecting *theoretical* promises.

"Go ahead and secure everything except ship to shore communications and the main search radar."

"Aye, aye, sir."

In the CIC Peter Christopher did not turn from his seat behind the main repeater operator. He put down the handset. "Everything off except the Type 965 and its repeaters," he declared. The rest of the team had been hanging on the edge of their seats waiting for the order. Screens started fading, the compartment grew dimmer. He listened to the reports, sighed with relief when the last one came in.

"EWO to bridge," he called, lifting the speaker handset to his face. "All non-essential search, targeting and communications gear has been secured."

For the first time in many minutes Peter Christopher became aware of the surging, bucking, violent progress of the destroyer across the stormy sea. Talavera was charging into the short, steep North Sea swells, and every now and then her propellers almost breached into thin air as she alternatively sliced through or rammed into each new wave, digging her bow deep one moment and racing forward, stern buried the next. If he had not been so terrified, he would probably have been being violently sea sick by now.

Chapter 7

Lieutenant-Commander Simon Collingwood guessed Dreadnought's cluttered pressure hull now sheltered at least two hundred souls. Most of her fitting out crew, some forty officers and men had reported to the boat within the first few minutes of the alarm being raised. Others, local dockyard workers, civilians, families from the bed and breakfast houses outside the dockyard gates, men from other ships, had quickly coalesced around the great beached whale in the main graving dock. When he saw the first lightning-like strike on the southern horizon Collingwood had a speaker mounted in the cockpit at the top of the submarine's sail and ordered everybody still above ground to come aboard Dreadnought.

The horrible quietness in the crush of bodies in the uncompleted nuclear submarine was punctuated by the cries of a baby, the occasional whispered order. Otherwise a fog of despair began to settle.

Collingwood stood by the periscope, sweeping the horizon with the scope set at minimum magnification with the red filter on the lens. He did not know if that would protect his sight if he happened to focus on the vicinity of a detonation. Right now, he was not sure if he cared. Nearby buildings and cranes obscured some ninety degrees of the eastern horizon so it was difficult to get accurate bearings of each successive strike and in any event, it was not a clear night. Heavy banks of cloud rolled over Furness, gaps in the overcast tended to be narrow, fleeting. It was like watching an intermittent distant firework display through a blindfold.

Albeit the most terrible firework display on earth.

He was scanning the northern sky when the whole world lit up like a nightmare.

"Fuck!" He muttered, tearing his face away from the eyepiece. He shook his head, blinked, discovering to his surprise that he was not blind. The periscope must have been pointed directly away from the airburst! "Count!" He demanded.

Eleven seconds later the blast over-pressure wave of the detonation across the other side of Morecombe bay smashed into the casing of HMS Dreadnought...

The thermonuclear warhead of the SS-5 medium range ballistic missile (MRBM) that detonated some seven miles due east of Dreadnought's dry dock at an altitude of two thousand feet, had a yield of 1.14 megatons. The missile was one of only a handful recently added to the inventory of the Soviet Strategic Missile Command and had been moved to an advanced base in Latvia just three weeks previously. The missile was so brand new that the units equipped with it had not yet fully familiarized themselves with its systems and operational parameters. Designed to strike targets up to 2,200 nautical miles distant with a circular error probability (CEP), of 0.5 miles, it had probably been targeted at a V-Bomber base in Yorkshire, or a centre of population such as Liverpool or Manchester, or perhaps, even the Vickers Industries Shipbuilders yard where HMS Dreadnought was known to be fitting out in preparation for her maiden voyage in the spring. Nobody would ever know its intended target although, self-evidently, it was reasonable to assume that the dead Soviet missile men who had launched it minutes before they themselves were swept to oblivion in a storm of thermonuclear fire, would not have had any reason to specifically target the middle of Morecambe Bay.

The fifty-million-degree ignition flash of the warhead lit up hundreds of square miles of sea, land and sky more brightly than any summer day in human history. The flash burned for over twenty seconds. Within ten seconds the fireball was a mile across and its temperature, although reduced by nearly eighty percent, still between ten and eleven million degrees. Anybody within twenty miles who had looked into the heart of the raging nuclear fire would have been blinded, and anybody out in the open within ten miles would have suffered second degree burns to exposed flesh.

The bomb that destroyed Hiroshima had exploded with a force equivalent to approximately 12,500 tons of Trinitrotoluene (TNT), or 0.0125 megatons. The bomb that detonated over Morecambe Bay that night had an explosive power of at least ninety times that of the Hiroshima bomb. If it had exploded on the ground it would have excavated a crater over one hundred feet deep and over a thousand feet in diameter. The walls of that crater, lethally irradiated, would have stood several stories high above the surrounding countryside, and the fast-rising mushroom cloud would have been heavily laden with pulverised soil and debris which would later return to earth, possibly hundreds of miles away as lethally radioactive fallout.

The Morecambe Bay bomb was, like the majority of the warheads deployed that night by all sides, configured to air burst. Unless a target was buried deep underground like a missile silo or a command bunker, or a specific runway or piece of vital 'hardened' infrastructure such as a dam or a port, a surface blast was the least efficient way to employ any nuclear weapon. An air burst was, all things being equal, at least twice as destructive as a ground blast and it sucked up significantly less radioactive fallout. Simply stated; in an air burst the *blast overpressure* created by the explosion is spread over a much wider area. In an environment where pinpoint accuracy cannot be relied upon, and where the initial blast and radiation cannot be guaranteed of itself to destroy a given target the great thermonuclear killer is *blast overpressure.*

Blast overpressure is a shock wave travelling at over seven hundred miles an hour, one mile every five seconds outwards in every direction from the epicentre of the blast. Two miles away from a one megaton air burst local overpressure is over ten pounds per square inch; every building is destroyed with only the traces of concrete foundations surviving. Within this radius of the explosion almost everybody is killed instantly. Four miles away, overpressure is 6 pounds per square inch, and everything above ground implodes or is blown away except the steel and concrete frames of buildings on the edge of the zone. An overpressure of 5 pounds will rupture eardrums, lungs, and transport a human body through the air like a rag doll in a two hundred mile an hour wind. Just 2 pounds of overpressure will flatten – literally *flatten* – a normal house. Between five and six miles away all windows will splinter explosively and hundred-mile-an-hour winds will blast into damaged buildings and scour the landscape. Ten miles away from the blast epicentre normal windows will disintegrate and rain deadly dagger-like slivers of glass onto anybody who has not taken shelter.

The mushroom cloud of a one megaton air burst ascends to fifteen or sixteen miles high, at which time it will be around thirty miles across. Within six miles nearly everybody will be dead or seriously injured, between six and ten miles perhaps twenty to thirty percent of people will be injured, and as many as ten percent as far out as ten to twenty miles. Anybody caught in the open out to the twenty-mile radius will probably have been killed or seriously injured and suffered first or second degree burns to exposed flesh; and anybody unfortunate enough to have been looking directly at the airburst will also be blinded for life.

On the eastern side of Morecombe Bay, the seaside town of Morecombe was wrecked, as was Lancaster several miles inland. The thermal pulse of the detonation ignited fires that quickly took hold in the ruins. In Morecombe the few survivors of the initial overpressure died trapped in the fires. In Lancaster, two to three miles inland, fires were slower to take hold and perhaps thirty percent of the population survived the first few days after the air burst. Down the coast Heysham was destroyed, north of Morecombe the village of Bolton-le-Sands and the town of Cairnforth were virtually wiped off the face of the earth. North of the air burst Cartmel, Flookburgh, Grange-over-Sands and practically every other sign of human habitation above ground ceased to exist, blown away by the fires from Hell. Ulveston, north-west of the air burst, and several communities on the Furness peninsular – by some fluke of thermodynamics – suffered less total destruction than places as close to the epicentre of the maelstrom to the east. In Ulveston some buildings still stood, fires did not take hold everywhere and perhaps fifty percent of the citizens survived the initial blast. Barrow began to burn within minutes of the air burst. In the dockyard debris rained across HMS Dreadnought's pressure casing like bullets.

In the crowded control room Lieutenant-Commander Simon Collingwood waited until the noise stopped. He rose to his feet and slowly turned, attempting to make eye contact with the terrified civilians, men, women and children and with his own people.

"Do we still have power from the external; generators?" He asked, wondering how he could be so calm.

"Yes, sir."

"Very good. We'll continue to charge our batteries while we can.

There were portable radiation monitors in the reactor compartment. For a moment until he thought better of it, he toyed with the idea of placing the devices near the open hatches.

No, let's not panic everybody quite yet.

There will be plenty to panic about soon enough.

Chapter 8

An extract from 'The Anatomy of Armageddon: America, Cuba, the USSR and the Global Disaster of October 1962' reproduced by the kind permission of the New Memorial University of California, Los Angeles Press published on 27th October 2012 in memoriam of the fallen.

We know what happened. Or do we? We have causality, an approximate timeline, and half-a-century of intensive military-industrial and academic research with which to deconstruct the catastrophe. But do we really know what happened?

Several key questions remain unresolved. Partly this is because many of the key documents on the American side are still classified and likely to so remain for at least another fifty years. Mainly, this is because America's allies – or more correctly, unwilling co-belligerents – have, over the years, wearied of the hand-wringing and the self-justifying politicking in Washington and in effect, withdrawn from the debate. For the Europeans, who after all bore the main cost of the seemingly absolute American – later pyrrhic – victory, until the question of culpability and reparations is unequivocally resolved there is nothing to discuss. Partly, there can be no definitive history of the October War because it was the only war in the modern age when a continental enemy was not defeated, but apparently annihilated.

Many in the United States of America blame what they interpret as societal 'moral disintegration' on the legacy of the war. Where, many ask, is the honour and the glory in celebrating, year after year, the extermination of an adversary that was so out-gunned? Would a super heavyweight boxer draw satisfaction from kneeling on a featherweight contender's chest and pummelling him until his head was a red and grey pulp on the canvass and splintered fragments of skull were showering down upon the front rows of the crowd? What kind of big fight audience would applaud that kind of pure bloody murder to the rafters?

Yes, the Soviets did fire the first shot.

Yes, the Soviets (or the Cubans, nobody knows who) subsequently launched three medium range ballistic missiles at the continental United States because they probably believed they were under attack.

So what? That is what the Europeans say and they have every right to ask it. Look at it from their perspective. A nuclear explosion in the sea north of Cuba destroys two American destroyers and badly damages a third. Let it not be forgotten that at the time those American destroyers were dropping depth charges – albeit practice ones – on a Soviet submarine *in international waters*.

In response to the sinking of their destroyers the American Navy and Air Force promptly scrambled scores of aircraft of all descriptions. It is unclear why they did this but panic and imbecility, rather than military calculation seem to have been the guiding martial principles invoked by senior US commanders on both land and at sea. Given that the Soviet and Cuban commanders, operating in a febrile operational climate that was even more paranoid than that of their American counterparts, suddenly saw their radar screens fill with enemy aircraft a reasonable person is bound to ask, what on the balance of probabilities were they likely to conclude? If you drive one's quarry into a corner is it surprising that he should come out fighting?

This is exactly what the Soviets (or the Cubans, or perhaps, both of them) did. At least one missile blew up on the launch pad. Three were successfully launched. Each missile was armed with a warhead with a yield of at least 1 megaton. One missile detonated on the ground thirteen miles north of Tampa, Florida. One air burst at an altitude of approximately seven thousand feet above the Gulf of Mexico some forty-three miles south east of New Orleans. One weapon air burst almost exactly equidistant from Galveston Island and Texas City, Houston.

The Tampa strike resulted in less than a thousand documented deaths and damaged or destroyed some twelve thousand properties. There were no reported fatalities related to the strike south east of New Orleans although several hundred persons suffered minor flash burns and recent dives on wrecks in the area suggest a number of vessels may have been sunk by the detonation. Both Galveston Island and Texas City were completely devastated by the third strike. Subsequent analysis showed that 96 percent of the people (over 74,000 souls) in those towns were killed in the initial air burst. The blast severely impacted the southern suburbs of Houston, where some 63,000 fatalities occurred in the first moments of the strike. Total casualties in the Houston area in the first thirty days after the strike were later estimated as 213,000 to 224,000 dead, and 307,000 injured.

It is at this point that the role of General Curtis LeMay, the legendary master builder of the Strategic Air Command (SAC) whom the Kennedy White House had inherited as the Chief of Staff of the US Air Force, becomes murky. When, in 1976, LeMay asked to appear before the standing Congressional Committee on the Causes and the Conduct of the Cuban War, he directly contradicted former Secretary of Defence, Robert S. McNamara's previously stated account of the counter strike against Cuba. In McNamara's version the White House ordered a retaliatory strike 'only against missile sites, air bases and major troop concentrations, avoiding where possible centres of population'. McNamara stated that the reasons for mandating a 'limited retaliatory strike were twofold: first, it was not believed that Cuban military personnel were capable of operating the SS4 MRBMs which had targeted Tampa and Galveston and therefore the blood of tens of thousands of Americans was mostly on the hands of the Kremlin rather than on the hands of the Cuban civilian population; and second, that a *comprehensive strike package* directed against Cuba risked exposing large areas of the southern United States and, or the rest of the Caribbean to unacceptably high levels of radioactive fallout'.

General LeMay, by then in retirement and embittered by his failed bids for the Presidency in 1968 and 1972, contemptuously dismissed McNamara's testimony, and that of other members of the Kennedy Administration. He was particularly scathing about remarks about his own part in the 'elimination of the Cuban menace for all time' and the concurrent decision to proceed with an all-out first strike against the Soviet Union and its Warsaw Pact allies consistent with the President's statement of 22nd October 1962', which had appeared in Robert Kennedy's recent book 'The Truth about the Cuban Crisis'. LeMay vociferously denied, not for the first time but for the first time unequivocally 'on the record' that his actions were driven by the receipt by coded protocol of the order to institute DEFCON 1. According to LeMay, President Kennedy had spoken to him by a secure telephone link and personally authorised him to execute *Plan Alpha*.

Then as now DEFCON 1 is that state of military readiness which assumes that nuclear war is imminent or that the continental United States is *already under nuclear attack* and requires all military forces to respond accordingly. Then as now *Plan Alpha* describes massive thermonuclear retaliation against whomsoever has or is about to attack the USA.

To his dying day General LeMay was unwavering in his insistence that on that fateful evening of Saturday 27th October 1962 he was obeying orders personally enunciated to him by his Commander-in-Chief.

No member of the Kennedy family attended LeMay's State Funeral in Washington. The feud over who actually pressed the 'Armageddon button' has raged for fifty years and neither the American people, or the citizens of the post-October War world know for sure what actually happened in Washington in the hours after the sinking of the USS Beale north of Cuba.

Nobody really knows if JFK's death bed last words really were: 'The mad sonofabitch killed eight hundred million people and tried to blame me!' The only thing we can know for certain is that none of the players on Capitol Hill that day foresaw *any* of the consequences of their machinations, consequences that would be the bane of their children, and the children of their children.

It matters little at this remove who said what to whom for when all is said and done that is a thing best left to historians. Cuba's nightmare fate was sealed. Within three hours of the Houston strike every city, town and area of settlement with a population of over five thousand, every suspected missile site, every port, every troop concentration on the island of Cuba had been targeted by at least two nuclear warheads. No inch of Cuban soil was not overlapped by simultaneous strikes. It is estimated that over 90 percent of the population of the island, over six million men, women and children died that day. When the first survey teams from the US Marine Corps arrived on Cuba forty days later, they discovered no living humans. Large areas of the island where ground bursts targeted suspected missile and air assets remain uninhabitable due to persistently high levels of irradiation to this day.

Cuba was but the sickening overture to what followed.

Once appraised of the motive to retaliate the genie – or in this case the great monster of retribution – was let out of its cage. That terrible monster ran wild for fourteen hours, fifty-seven minutes and approximately thirty-four seconds and in that time committed an atrocity unparalleled in human history.

While a rational case can be made for a relatively limited retaliation against *specific* objectives in Cuba, had it been conducted in such as way so as to not annihilate all sentient life on that island, this author, in common with the majority of historians who have addressed these dreadful matters in the last half-century, can find no good – or sane – justification for the massive and inevitably overwhelming assault on the military, economic and social fabric of the Soviet Union and its allies.

The unimaginable human cost of this attack and the totally unnecessary catastrophe it inflicted on the European allies of the United States of America ought, long before now, to have made of this country an international pariah for all time. This may yet come to pass and for this reason I make no apology for restating the cold, hard facts behind Armageddon.

Had the Kennedy Administration held its nerve Nikita Khrushchev would have had no alternative but to back down; in fact there is evidence that he was in the process of doing exactly that as the first ICBMs ignited over Moscow and the as the first wave of B-52s pulverised Murmansk, Leningrad, Vladivostok Riga and Kiev. Had the Kennedy Administration offered Khrushchev so much as a crumb of comfort – say an undertaking that at some unspecified future date the removal of the obsolete Thor medium range missiles stationed in Turkey – to soften the pill, the Cuban Missile Crisis would have been just that. A crisis like most crises; resolved by realpolitik diplomacy. This was not a situation analogous to the comedy of errors played out by that imbecilic rag tag bunch of in bred, megalomaniac European princelings and their lap dog retainers in the summer of 1914. Nuclear war was not inevitable in October 1962 and crucially, neither of the main protagonists was under any real illusion as to the likely outcome of such a war.

The Kennedy Administration possessed intelligence that US forces alone – that is, without taking into account the 150 plus strong British V-Bomber Force – had a strategic intercontinental first strike capability that was between six and eight times that of the Soviets. This CIA assessment was broadly correct other than in terms of the actual scale of the American advantage. On paper we now know that US Forces alone actually enjoyed a 'capability advantage' of approximately seventeen to one over their enemy.

In the Kremlin, Khrushchev *knew* that the Strategic Missile forces under his command had virtually *no* viable first strike capability against *any* target located in the continental United States. That was, after all, *why* the Politburo had so badly wanted to base a hundred SS-4 medium range ballistic missiles (MRBMs) with a range of 1,300 miles on Cuba in the first place in an foolhardy attempt to *level the playing field* and forestall the day when the perfidious Americans would wake up, smell the coffee, and exploit their overwhelming strategic power. Seen through the prism of the paranoia of those Cold War years, had the Soviets been able to base SS-4s on Cuba in the same way the USA had already based Thor MRBMs in Turkey and the United Kingdom, from the point of view of the Kremlin the world might, conceivably, have seemed a much safer place.

After all, it was only because it believed this that the fateful decision to mount *Operation Anadyr* – the *Cuban Option* – had been taken in the first place.

Chapter 9

Walter Brenckmann discovered later that the 1.2 megaton warhead of the Soviet ICBM – probably targeted on central Boston – had overshot its target by as many as ten miles to air burst at one thousand five hundred feet above the town of Quincy. Quincy was the birthplace of two former American Presidents, John Adams and John Quincy Adams, a city in its own right but for over half-a-century a feeder commuter suburb of the Boston metropolitan area to its north along the curve of Quincy Bay where it merged into Boston Bay. Ninety-nine percent of its population of over seventy thousand souls died in the first second after the explosion, the few survivors who got down to their basements and cellars in time, died in the next few seconds, burned and crushed in the ruins. Momentarily the annihilating fifty-million-degree bloom of the airburst consumed Weymouth to the south, its thermal pulse flashing across and firing the southern suburbs of the great city to the north like the blowtorch of the gods. The firestorm scoured the surface of the Bay of all life for several miles out to sea before the tsunami shockwave of blast overpressure smashed into the southern suburbs and the port of Boston.

The flash turned night to day eleven-and-a-half nautical miles away in Cambridge as Walter Brenckmann bundled his complaining wife,

Joanne, through the basement door and followed her down the flight of steps into the concrete sanctuary beneath the old house. The room had been the kids' playground in the New England winters of their childhood; latterly it had become the family utility room. Washing machine, tumble dryer, a big Westinghouse larder fridge stood against one wall. Against another wall was a work bench with tools lying untidily on its top, a chair that Walter had been attempting to repair perched atop it amid wood scrapings. The old, threadbare living room sofa they had replaced upstairs three years ago sat in the middle of the cold room. It was bitterly cold because they did not bother turning on the heating now the kids were gone.

"What was that?" Joanne asked as the lights flickered.

Her husband did not reply as he calmly searched his toolbox for a torch.

The lights flickered again and then all was dark.

"Walter?"

"The electro-magnetic pulse of a big bomb trips the nearest transformers, after that the local power grid shorts out," her husband explained, gently, patiently. He switched on the torch, pointed it at Joanne's feet, then towards the sofa. "We ought to sit down and wait."

"Wait for what, Walter?"

The end of the world.

What he actually said was: "To see if the power comes back on, sweetheart."

Together they settled on the sofa and drew the blankets they had snatched from the airing cupboard on their way down to the bottom of the house around themselves.

Joanne leaned against her husband.

"Are you as scared as I am, honey?"

I'm so scared I'm surprised I haven't evacuated my bowels!

"Naw," Walter Brenckmann drawled, "we've done what we can do, sweetheart. The rest is in God's hands."

They were both Sunday Baptists. Neither were true believers. Their chapel, St Mark's, had been the centre of their social orbit for some years, the congregation largely comprised couples like themselves, with kids in common, schools in common, jobs in the nearby city in common, with Democratic politics in common, and so on...

The house seemed to shudder, sway.

The sound of breaking, falling glass on bare boards seemed deafening.

For a moment they held their breath, expecting the whole building to crash down on top of them.

"I love you, Jo," Walter said.

His wife snuggled closer.

"I've always loved you, Walt. Always and forever."

"Always and forever," her husband repeated, kissing the top of her head.

Chapter 10

What was going on?

Marija Calleja peered across the wide neck of Sliema Creek into the blackness of Marsamxett Harbour towards the looming bastion walls of the fortress city of Valletta. Only the bow and stern lights of the warships and the waving fingers of light from hand held lamps illuminated the dark waters. Her eyes had quickly adjusted to the night. Launches and whalers plied between the big ships as they raised steam. In their anxiety to get out to sea their boilers were burning unusually noxious, acrid plumes of smoke into the clear Mediterranean air.

Panic.

No, not *panic*, but the next best thing.

What was going on?

The air raid sirens wailed in the distance but nobody knew where they were supposed to go. The war had been over for seventeen years and the old shelters had been barred and locked years ago. After the war people had lived in some of the caves beneath the citadel of Valletta and the ruins of the Three Cities - Vittoriosa, Senglea and Cospicua - for years until, finally, the ruins were demolished, new housing built and where possible, wrecked buildings repaired. Under a cool, cloudless, star-filled sky the ships of the 7th Destroyer Squadron were desperately lighting off their boilers.

HMS Scorpion must have been the squadron duty ship with at least one, possibly both of her boilers primed or minimally fired and ready for movement at less than two hours' notice otherwise she would never have had sufficient steam to have cleared the anchorage so swiftly. Scorpion was already out of sight beyond Tigne Point. The next destroyer, HMS Aisne was only now starting to move. This vessel was an earlier sister ship of Peter Christopher's Talavera, in silhouette *he said* a perfect mirror image of her *pen friend's* ship. *Pen friend?* That sounded so inadequate it was ridiculous, Marija chided her girlish other self. But how else was she to think of Peter, a man of approximately her own age with whom she had corresponded since she was eleven years old? No man would ever know her as well as Peter Christopher knew her; and she hoped that no woman would ever know him as she knew him. So how should she think, speak or dream of him on a night like this when something so strange and frightening was happening all around her?

A tug's whistle repeatedly blared a warning.

HMS Aisne seemed for a moment as if she might drift broadside on against the persistent south easterly wind blowing down the length of Sliema Creek. Then a tug moved under her port bow and in a mad churning of the shallow waters pushed the destroyer's head around to face towards Valletta.

"The British are scared of something," Marija Calleja's twenty-two-year-old brother Joseph declared, grinning. Joe worked in the docks at

Senglea when he was not on strike or organising demonstrations against the 'occupying power'.

Marija folded her arms, hugging herself as if there was a sudden chill in the air in the balmy Mediterranean night.

Brother and sister stood in the road looking down to the harbour.

In the distance the red-hot jet pipes of jets taking off from the RAF base at Luqa climbed into the night, the rushing thunder of their engines falling down to the ground like some ill omen from the gods.

"Don't you think that if 'the British' are afraid of something," Marija suggested, unaccountably vexed by her little brother's smug complacency, "that perhaps, we ought to be also?"

This thought had not occurred to Joseph Calleja.

"Why?" He asked before he switched on his brain.

"The British have hundreds of soldiers, they have jet fighters and bombers and big grey warships with guns and space age missiles," she reminded her brother patiently. "Why would they be afraid of anything?"

"Ah..."

Chapter 11

Lieutenant-Commander Simon Collingwood had donned an anti-flash balaclava, pulled on a Parka and climbed up the ladder to the small cockpit on top of HMS Dreadnought's great shark fin sail. He expected another airburst any moment but he felt, in his bones, that he needed to *see*, with his own eyes, what was going on. It simply was not the same *seeing* it through the periscope.

There were two small fires near the northern dockyard gate and more, larger fires in the town beyond. Within the Vickers Armstrong Industries Yard, the brilliant arc lighting was off although here and there the standard pole lights survived. There was dust and grit in the wet air, he could taste it. In the middle distance he saw hand torches weaving through dockyard machinery. He stared hard at the access ways and roads around Dreadnought's graving dock. They were strewn with small pieces of debris, otherwise clear. There were no bodies on the ground within his field of vision and he sighed with relief.

His relief was short-lived.

There were big fires flickering distantly across Morecambe Bay. Heysham, Lancaster, Cairnthorpe, places he knew well would have been hit hard. He tried to get his mind into gear. It was not easy; he was too numbed to the core with the terrifying enormity of the disaster. The bomb must have airburst somewhere over the Bay several miles away or he would not still be here. None of them would still be here if it had gone off much closer.

Collingwood snatched the trailing bridge microphone, clicked it on.

"Can you hear me down there?"

There was a burr of static.

"Yes, sir," acknowledged the man at the talker station in the crowded control room over forty feet beneath Collingwood's feet.

"Everything is still intact up here. I want the galley up and running. I'm sure our guests would appreciate tea or hot chocolate. Somebody can bring me a flask of tea when that's organised."

"Aye, aye, sir."

Collingwood was amazed at how calm he sounded.

Given that his pulse was racing and that under his layers of protective clothing he was sweating like a pig despite the frost of the night, he did not know how he could possibly sound *that* calm.

The horrors of nuclear war had seemed so banal, surreal a year ago at the staff college course that he and the other prospective members of Dreadnought's wardroom cadre had attended at Devonport.

'We think the most likely scenario is that both sides will shoot themselves dry as fast as they can,' the chief instructor had concluded. 'Basically, once the thing kicks off there's no point holding fire. You either hit the other fellow with everything you've got as soon as you can or you lose. So, we might be talking about a war that's over in hours, twelve or twenty-four bar a few afterthoughts. The aggressor's first strike, and whatever counter strike the non-aggressor can mount while under attack. That's it. After the first strike command and control doesn't exist. After the first strike everybody goes underground, under the sea, or if you're on a surface vessel, as far out to sea as you can get as fast as you can hoping to lose yourself in the vastness of the world's oceans...'

Except you couldn't do any of those things if you were on board a ninety-five percent complete nuclear submarine that was sitting in a dry dock!

Simon Collingwood did not know how long *this* real, hot war was going to last. The one thing he *could not* afford to assume was that it was already over. His mind was ticking through the possibilities, the practicalities. He had two hundred people sheltering on his boat. In the morning there would be more. They had to be fed, watered, sustained, protected. By *him*. Until somebody told him otherwise, they were his responsibility now that the world had gone mad.

He clicked the microphone switch.

"Captain to talker."

"Yes, sir."

"Put me on tannoy." Collingwood waited for the acknowledgement. "This is Simon Collingwood, acting Captain of Dreadnought. I'd like to welcome aboard all non-Dreadnoughts. The situation topside looks a little grim but there haven't been any further big bangs since that last one which appears to have been over open water in the middle of Morecambe Bay." *Try not to be too bloody cheerful man!* "Right now, you are in the safest place. Dreadnought's pressure hull is like several inches of armour plating," which was a complete lie, "so what we're going to do is sit this thing out until we know it is safe to go back outside. It is dark up here but there is enough light to be able to tell that the town of Barrow is still intact. I daresay a lot of windows have been broken but everything still seems to be standing. This is one of those times when we all need to stick together. While you remain on Dreadnought, I am responsible for your safety. Please stay calm. Everybody, please stay calm. If there is any fresh news, I promise I will pass it on to you as soon as I can. Captain, out."

Collingwood heard a sound behind him and a bulky figure in a parka and white balaclava like his own emerged from the open hatch at his feet.

Lieutenant Richard Manville, Dreadnought's Supply Officer, was a clumsy, generously-proportioned man of around six feet in height. Submariners tended to be smaller, wiry men like Collingwood himself but Dick Manville was one of the new breed of University educated, short-commission – seven- or thirteen-year men rather than 'lifers' like Collingwood - entrants to the underwater club.

"Well said, sir," the newcomer declared, breathlessly as he straightened to his full height in the cramped cockpit. "The Chief asked me to tell you we have thirty-six Dreadnoughts on board, and one hundred and eighty-one assorted guests, including thirty-two youngsters under the age of twelve. We've got enough fresh water for a couple of mugs of tea for everybody but not a lot else in the larder, I'm afraid, sir."

Collingwood grimaced under his balaclava.

"I don't want any foraging parties going ashore until it is fully light, Dick." He eyed the malevolent night around the sail. "Or until such time as the whiz bangs have stopped."

The younger man was staring at the fires in the town.

"Understood, sir."

"I'm going to come below in about ten minutes. Get the Chief to organise a relief up here." Collingwood was thinking ahead. He needed to be seen in the crowded spaces of the boat, to be a visibly calming presence. Then he needed to be making plans to get Dreadnought out of this dock and taking her somewhere where *she would be safe.*

Chapter 12

05:35 Hours (04:35 Hours GMT)
Sliema-Gzira Waterfront, Malta

Marija Calleja and her brother Joe had walked down to the waterfront. She had wrapped in a shawl over her coat, he was just wearing his tattered and torn dockyard monkey jacket over his grubby work clothes. They sat on the sea wall, swinging their feet, watching the black silhouettes of the darkened warships desperately raising steam, crabbing out of Sliema Creek. Across the water on the tip of Manoel Island the Headquarters of the Royal Navy's Mediterranean Fleet was a ferment of dark noise. HMS Phoenicia sat inside the great medieval fortress walls first raised by the Knights of St John overlooking both Marsamxett and Sliema Creeks.

A consequence of Marija's childhood and adolescence mostly spent in hospital was that she was inordinately well read by the standards of her peers. Everybody thought she was the most bookish of women, a mine of useless information, in fact. However, there were compensations. For example, on a night like this she could fall into the well of her thoughts and contemplate the history and the traditions of her people drawing on an unusual wealth of background *facts*.

"I wonder if the British would have put their headquarters on Manoel Island if they'd known that originally it was Malta's plague island?" She asked out aloud, baiting her little brother to say something nonsensical.

"Best place for them!" Her sibling retorted. He opened his mouth to continue but tonight the unreality of what was going on had unsettled him to the point where he did not know what to think anymore.

Marija let it go in silence, swiftly falling back into her thoughts.

Manoel Island had originally been called *l'Isola del Vescovo* or, in Maltese, *il-Gżira tal-Isqof* which translated roughly as 'the Bishop's Island'. And so it had remained until post medieval times when in 1643 Jean Paul Lascaris, Grandmaster of the Knights of Malta, had built a quarantine hospital – a lazaretto - on the island, in response to the periodic waves of plague and cholera brought to Malta by visiting ships. The island had not obtained its modern name until the 18th century, renamed in honour of António Manoel de Vilhena, a Portuguese Grandmaster of the Knights of Malta under whose leadership the original Fort Manoel was built in 1726. At the time the fort was a marvel of 18th century military engineering. Some uncertainty existed as to the guiding hand behind the original plans for the structure. However, the general consensus was that the grand plan was the work of one Louis d'Augbigne Tigné, somewhat modified by his friend Charles François de Mondion. The latter was actually buried in a crypt beneath the fort. Bombed repeatedly by the Luftwaffe in the early 1940s Fort Manoel – currently named HMS Phoenicia - retained its impressive internal quadrangle parade ground and arcade. The baroque chapel of St. Anthony of Padua within the fort's walls had been almost totally destroyed by bombing in March 1942 but had subsequently been rebuilt as the base chapel, albeit not quite in the magnificent style of its pre-German war pomp.

Some ten minutes ago the brother and sister had gazed at the tall, threatening, elegant bulk of a British cruiser feeling its way past the rocks at the foot of Manoel Island and the seaward end of Tigne Point. Now HMS Broadsword, the last of the 7th Destroyer Squadron's big beasts was finally moving. The dirty, sulphurous waft of smoke from her thin rear stack blew down the length of the Gzira waterfront.

Valletta across the water was still in total darkness.

There were soldiers with rifles on the streets and sailors trying to jump on the last boats back to their ships, hundreds of civilians like the brother and sister milling, aimlessly, sleepily as army trucks spilled away from the nearby Cambridge barracks vehicle pool.

Marija gazed at HMS Broadsword. With her tall forward lattice mast, big bedstead radar and strange thin second funnel she lacked the lithe grace and greyhound lines of so many of the British destroyers that she had seen in Sliema Creek over the years.

In years gone by she and Joe had often come down to the Creek, sat on the sea wall swinging their feet, killing time, teasing each other. They had always been the closest of the three Calleja siblings, sharing the same dry, mischievous sense of humour. Tonight, in the minutes before the first hint of the pre-dawn twilight the skies above the island were full of jet engines. The roar buffeted their senses, making the whole world reverberate.

A British soldier rested the butt of his rifle on the ground a few paces to Marija's right. She heard the scratch of a match, a flame flared as the man lit a cigarette.

"Excuse me," she asked. "Do you know what's going on, sir?"

"I ain't no 'sir', love," the man chuckled, stepping closer. Like so many of the men posted to Malta this man had a very British gruff affability, as if he knew he was mostly among friends even if lately, there had been rumblings and outbreaks of hostility. It was unusual even for those Maltese who most fervently wanted the British to go home to harbour any real personal animosity towards individual soldiers, sailors or airmen. "As for 'what's going on', your guess is as good as mine."

"Why all the guns, Tommy?" Joe Calleja inquired, without the mocking edge he'd have injected if he'd been at a Maltese Labour Party rally, or on the picket line outside the gates of Senglea Dockyard.

"Tommy?" The soldier guffawed.

"My brother has no manners," Marija apologised in a tone of voice that let the other man know that she was scowling ferociously at her sibling.

"No offence taken, love," the soldier assured her. He leaned his rifle, a black metalled FN L1A1 SLR on the sea wall next to the woman. He positioned himself with several feet between him and the siblings, and sucked on his cigarette as he stared at HMS Broadsword slowly creeping past. "No offence," he repeated. "Don't ask me what I'm doing here. All I know is that this is a better billet than Mönchengladbach on a winter's night like this."

"Mönchengladbach?" Marija asked, a smile quirking her lips and brightening her voice in the night.

"Second Battalion got posted to Mönchengladbach in Germany. My lot got sent to the Med. My company to here, the other two to Akrotiri. That's Cyprus. Most of my lot are either in Germany right now, or dodging petrol bombs from terrorists in Cyprus. Me, I'm here in what ought to be a little piece of paradise. Once in a while somebody gets a bit snotty, like your young man, here. But me and my mates know even the snotty ones don't really mean anything by it."

"He is my little brother," Marija confessed.

"No accounting for family," the man sympathised, taking another drag on his cigarette.

"You really don't know what's going on then?"

"I know it ain't no exercise."

"My name is Marija," she volunteered spontaneously.

"I'm Jim Siddall," the soldier replied, touching his brow with the back of a hand shielding his cigarette.

Marija saw for the first time that the man was in his thirties with sergeant's stripes on his arm. She waved into the gloom in her brother's direction.

"This is my brother Joe."

"Yes, I know." Another chuckle, utterly lacking in malice. "We'll arrest him another night, perhaps." Marija was about to morph into wounded tigress defending her brood mode when the sergeant went on. "Just make sure you keep him out of harm's way tonight. People are a bit trigger happy tonight. So, you take care, Miss Calleja."

Marija looked up at him as he got to his feet.

"What is going on, Sergeant Siddall?"

"I don't know, love," he said, his face illuminated by the red glow of his cigarette. "For all I know it's the end of the world."

Chapter 13

An extract from 'The Anatomy of Armageddon: America, Cuba, the USSR and the Global Disaster of October 1962' reproduced by the kind permission of the New Memorial University of California, Los Angeles Press published on 27th October 2012 in memoriam of the fallen.

While it would be completely wrong to blame the catastrophe on a cabal of senior American military officers - gathered around General Curtis Lemay - who believed that the Cuban crisis was a dangerous symptom of growing Soviet nuclear bravura, there was an awareness in the Pentagon, and elsewhere in the Washington intelligentsia that the atomic dominance enjoyed by the USA since 1945 was coming to an end. Whether we can extrapolate this 'feeling' among the decision making caucus in and around the Kennedy White House, into a pre-disposition that if there was to be a war then it was better to have that war while America still held the advantage - or a belief that such a war might still be in some meaningful way 'winnable' - is unclear, and inevitably much of the byzantine politicking beneath the surface will remain opaque forever.

Oh, to have been a fly on the wall at JKF or his brother, Robert's confessionals! Rumours of secret journals and memoirs penned by key members of the

Kennedy Administration have tormented historians for decades; they may exist but are unlikely to see the light of day while any of the key players or their close family relatives is still alive. Without them we must work with the sources that we have, and these are limited. Remember, the Cuban Missile Crisis that spawned the October War and unleashed so much grief down the years since happened in an age before ubiquitous email and SMS traffic, when paper trails were exactly that – paper trails – relatively easily edited, amended or in extremis, burned or shredded as dictated by political circumstances.

It may be significant that thus far nobody has managed to get their hands on a 'smoking gun'. There may not actually be a 'smoking gun'. In the absence of a 'smoking gun' we cannot, at this remove, prove that JFK, or any of the other key decision makers fully realised the massive strategic nuclear strike superiority of Western forces over their Soviet counterparts. Likewise, because the paper trail is so scratchy – whether by design or accident – we cannot say for certain that if they had fully understood their position of overwhelming strategic superiority, it would have changed anything.

Whilst this author has always been sceptical about the more Machiavellian manoeuvrings attributed to Curtis Lemay that fateful weekend in October 1962; this author wishes to make it crystal clear that she does not subscribe to the simple-minded, neo-determinist view that John F. Kennedy deliberately went to war because he believed it was the last best chance of destroying the Red Menace once and for all time. JFK was no angel. He was the womanising, playboy, drug addicted son of a ruthless and immensely wealthy tycoon. Years after his death we discovered JFK suffered from Addison's disease. Throughout his Presidency he was wracked with agonising back and joint pain, he was often incontinent, high on pain killers. Nevertheless, the verdict of history is that he was plainly not, *per se,* a bad man. For all that he came from a family legendary for its mendacity, he was – no more than Curtis LeMay – Machiavelli reincarnated. Both before and after the war JFK's Presidency was punctuated with charismatic leadership, real moral courage, and a deeply held commitment to the rights of *all* Americans. He wanted his children to grow up in a better, fairer, more peaceful world. There might have been men around him advocating a devastating first strike but John Fitzgerald Kennedy would never, under any circumstances, have authorised it *just because he could.*

We shall come back to exactly why JFK unleashed the hounds of Hell later. First let us examine the actual balance of terror in October 1962. In this examination the author asks American readers to remember one thing, and one thing only. JFK and his inner circle might not have fully comprehended the true threat posed to the USA and its allies by Soviet nuclear forces, but he and his advisors knew – to within a few tens of megatons – the true capability of his own forces.

Strategic Nuclear Capability

To avoid confusion this author defines *Strategic Nuclear* Capability as being one side's ability to strike at the other's continental mass.

Given that it is tempting to be seduced by purely statistical methods of accounting, the numbers need to be qualified. Not so much because the raw numbers fail to convey the crushing superiority of US Forces – because they do – but because, they tend to significantly *under estimate* the *totality* of the strategic overkill represented by those forces.

US weapon systems were more technologically advanced, accomplished and reliable than their Soviet counterparts, and the day to day combat readiness of the same was much higher on the US side. Likewise, US delivery systems were more numerous, more varied and stationed all around the Soviet Union. US command and control systems were also inherently superior and more effective than their Soviet counterparts.

There was only one area in which Soviet preparations for nuclear war were markedly superior to those in the United States, or any of its allies; and that was in the sphere of civil defence. However, since a full-scale civil defence mobilisation in the middle of a crisis would have been a clear signal to the Kennedy Administration that the Soviets were contemplating a first strike, no such mobilisation actually took place and therefore, Soviet planning in this area was never tested.

By October 1962 the US had a stockpile of over 26,000 nuclear weapons and the Soviets some 3,300. Of these weapons the US had around 3500 weapons on quick alert status, or ready for immediate activation which could be targeted on the Soviet Union, whereas the Soviets had less than 250 which could, theoretically, be targeted on the continental USA.

On Saturday 27th October 1962 the Soviets had no more than 42 Inter-Continental Ballistic Missiles (ICMBs), of which less than two-thirds were operational. The remainder of the Soviet Union's strategic nuclear strike capability was comprised of a force of some 160 long-range Bear and Bison heavy bombers each capable of carrying one or two free fall bombs.

According to the *Official History of the Strategic Air Command, Volume II, 1962 to 1964* published in 1987, SAC had 2,907 'fully generated' nuclear weapons to hand on the day of the war. Of these, 1,528 were on 'quick alert' status (that is, ready for immediate deployment). These weapons were distributed between 160 silo based operational ICBMs, and a long-range strategic bomber force equipped with B-47s and B-52s. On that day, as on every day in that period, at least sixteen 'bombed up' B-52s were in the air at any one-time flying missions to fail safe points short of Soviet territory, or loitering out of range of enemy radar over the Arctic, the North Pacific, or the Indian Oceans. In those days when the first Polaris submarines were only recently entering service, the 600 B-52s of SAC were like loaded guns permanently held at the head of the Soviet leadership.

The Truman and Eisenhower Administrations had poured untold treasure into the creation of SAC, bequeathing to their successor, John Fitzgerald Kennedy the instrument of Armageddon. In comparison the Soviet bomber force had been designed to frighten the West, and little else. Its most advanced component, the Myasishchev M-4 Molot (NATO codename Bison) was a four-engine jet bomber significantly less capable and advanced than any of its American of British counterparts. The Tupolev Tu-95 (NATO codename Bear) was a four-engine *turboprop* bomber. Both aircraft had first flown in the early fifties and neither had been produced in large numbers. It is unlikely that more than a hundred – perhaps fifty of each type – were combat ready on 27th October 1962. Unlike SAC, the Soviets lacked the resources, or the confidence to maintain a round the clock airborne strike force.

Both the Americans and the Soviets had been progressively building up their local and continental air defence systems. The North American Aerospace Defence Command (NORAD), jointly set up by the USA and Canada had already turned the air space between Alaska in the west and Newfoundland in the east into a vast aerial killing ground. There was as yet no NORAD defence against ICBM strikes, but any unauthorised aircraft straying into Canadian or North America airspace would almost certainly be destroyed long before reaching the major cities of either nation. Soviet air defences were less sophisticated but increasingly potent, comprising layered radar and missile belts and large numbers of interceptors. However, the Soviet air defence system was strongest opposite Europe, whereas the biggest threat came from SAC bombers attacking over the Arctic or from the fastnesses of the North Pacific, or from the south over the Himalayas.

It is estimated that perhaps as many as forty Bears and Bisons attempted to attack North American targets. None of them breached NORAD's kill zone. All fourteen successful nuclear strikes on Canadian and United States territory were by ICBMs (three launched from Cuba in the first phase of the exchange, and eleven launched from the Soviet Union in the minutes before, or during the US's so-called 'retaliatory strike').

Before the October War the CIA had believed the US had a strategic nuclear advantage of at least six to one. The Soviets believed that they had a *disadvantage* of at least seventeen to one. In terms of the actual weight of the attack US forces (and their allies) delivered on targets in the Soviet Union, in practice, the US and its allies, demonstrated a first strike advantage of approximately 100 to 150 to one.

In addition to SAC, the US had other strategic nuclear strike assets located around the world. The United States Navy's Atlantic Command had seven Polaris-armed ballistic missile submarines based at Holy Loch in Scotland. Notwithstanding that the early models of their submarine launched missiles were as unreliable as the Soviets' land-based ICBMs these seven boats carried 112 SLBMs with sufficient range to hit Moscow from a firing position one hundred feet beneath the surface of the Norwegian Sea. Pacific Command had eight SSM-N-8A Regulus and 16 MACE cruise missiles capable of striking targets deep inside Asiatic Russia. There were also three fleet aircraft carriers, each carrying up to forty nuclear weapons, and another fifty free fall weapons available to shore based bombers.

It was only in the European theatre of operations that Soviet forces had any kind of parity. There were between four and five thousand US nuclear weapons in Europe but the majority were designated for battlefield use, 155- and 203-mm artillery shells, land mines, or air space denial short range surface-to-air missiles. In terms of weapons which could hit targets in the Soviet Union, European Command had 105 Thor and Jupiter missiles based in the UK and Turkey, 48 Mace cruise missiles, two Sixth Fleet aircraft carriers in the Mediterranean with a combined throw of around eighty weapons, and elsewhere in Europe around fifty free fall bombs deliverable by American aircraft.

This calculation took no regard for the RAF V-Bomber force of about 150 sophisticated long-range four-engine bombers based on the East Coast of England. While the RAF did not routinely fly failsafe missions along SAC lines, a proportion of its Vulcans, Valiants and Victors was constantly on QRA (quick reaction alert) at the end of their runways, fuelled and bombed up and ready to go at four minutes notice.

If the Soviets lacked a viable strategic first strike capability against the United States, the scales of the

European balance of terror were rather more closely aligned. In October 1962 the Soviets had some five hundred SS-4s and SS-5s, medium range ballistic missiles with approximate ranges of 1,300 and 2,200 miles respectively. It is not known how many of these assets were based in Europe and how many were based in the east, threatening targets in the Pacific. Notwithstanding that a similar number of Soviet missiles struck targets in both east (in China) and west (in Europe), it is postulated that the split was probably 75-25 (with a much larger number of missiles being destroyed on the ground in Europe than in Asia due to the concentrated, carpet bombing tactics applied in the west.

It was entirely predictable that in the event of an all-out nuclear exchange that the greater part of any 'collateral damage' suffered by NATO would inevitably be in Europe.

Whatever else the movers and shakers in Washington knew about the strategic balance of terror; the virtual destruction of Western Europe was a given.

However, even now, fifty years later, there are senior politicians and shapers of opinion who - flying in the face of the fact of history - deny this.

Chapter 14

09:15 Hours (08:15 Hours GMT)
Monday 29th October 1962
St Catherine's Hospital for Women, Rabat-Mdina,
Malta

That morning Marija Calleja had left the house just after seven o'clock and walked down the gentle slope to the bus stop on the Gzira waterfront overlooking the eerily empty anchorage of Sliema Creek.

The big, predatory grey silhouettes of the ships of the 7th Destroyer Squadron had not returned to their anchorage in the sheltered blue waters of the Creek. Neither had the minesweepers or the ungainly LSTs (Landing Ship Tanks) usually moored in the shallower water nearer the sea wall or at the end of the Royal Marines' embarkation jetty on Manoel Island. Over twenty-four hours later the semi-organised panic and commotion of the early hours of Sunday morning had been replaced with an atmosphere of horribly uneasy calm. There were unsmiling armed men in Naval and Army uniforms on the sea wall and directing traffic and in the sky jet engines quartered the heavens.

Marija's mother had pleaded with her to stay at home.

Radio Malta was playing patriotic music and asking everybody to 'keep calm' every fifteen minutes. It had been announced that there would be a dusk to dawn curfew the coming evening. *A state of martial law had been declared.* Marija did not know what that meant; just that it sounded very bad.

Her little brother, Joe, had started complaining about 'British Imperialist oppression' and declared that the 'proletariat should stand up to the English bully boys." She had given him what she hoped was a withering look, told him not to be stupid and to go to work as normal.

"Will the buses be running?" Her mother had demanded in her most plaintive of tones.

"I don't know," she'd retorted. "But if they are, I will go to work. *As normal!*"

It was often remarked upon how the myriad of little things that seemed to dominate other people's lives left Marija Calleja untouched, and that she had an uncanny knack of serenely breezing through the day to day minor tribulations that tripped up practically everybody else. It was not true, of course. It was simply that she had decided, many years ago that her 'life cup' was always going to be half full, rather than half empty.

At the waterfront bus stop opposite Triq It Torri – the road that climbed the hill at a right angle to the harbour and cut across the base of the Tigne Peninsula linking Gzira with the Sliema - Marija had discovered that the buses were running normally. The buses were not actually running on time, or with any particular reference to the printed timetables, but the buses were running, more or less, *normally* by the lights of buses on Malta. That morning, *normal* felt very strange and the crowd at the bus stop was unusually subdued, a nod or a terse 'hello' passed for greetings whereas before the weekend conversations would have flowed, possibly volubly.

It was a bright, sunny late October morning and few people wore coats. The last air raid siren had shut down a little after six o'clock yesterday morning and afterwards the streets had filled with people spilling out of basements. There had been nothing to see except the empty anchorages of Marsamxett, and Sliema and Lazaretto Creeks and the starry sky slowly turning to grey with the new dawn.

Marija settled in a window seat on the left-hand side of the bus as it rumbled around the harbour following the sea wall, past the entrance bridge – now heavily barricaded – to the headquarters of the British Mediterranean Fleet on Manoel Island. As the bus turned left and dragged painfully around the corner Marija saw that Lazaretto Creek – customarily crowded with vessels of all sizes - was almost as empty as Sliema Creek. Apart from the big, slab-sided accommodation and depot ship HMS Maidstone and a single destroyer – HMS Cassandra - moored alongside all the big ships were gone. Further along she got her first sight down the length of Marsamxett where the destroyers came to take on oil and ammunition. Accustomed to spying the long, low shark-like silhouettes of as many as half-dozen submarines sheltering under the ramparts of Fort Manoel it was a little unnerving to see the whole length of the anchorage completely empty. All the big ships that could raise steam and the submarines were gone.

At the circus-shaped bus station outside the citadel gates to Valletta she stepped off one bus onto another, which sat twenty minutes on its stand while the driver smoked two cigarettes and conversed loudly in Maltese spiced with ribald pigeon English with his friends. Eventually, the bus set off down the gentle incline into war-scarred Floriana. She remembered travelling this same route as a child. In those days it had seemed to her that every other building was in ruin. Rubble from that war was still piled in great mounds, in summer the pulverized stone dust blew across the streets like swirling sandy dirt devils every time the wind gusted from the south west. The rebuilding had only really begun in the last few years and in many areas the old wounds were as yet, hardly less raw than they had been twenty years ago.

The scandal of the snail like pace of the reconstruction was the one thing she and Joe agreed about. Ever since the war the British had populated Malta's anchorages with warships - expensive castles of steel - and filled the Maltese Archipelago's skies with modern jet aircraft that seemed like machines straight out of futuristic science fiction comics; and yet the pace of rebuilding and reconstruction was maddeningly slow. In flaunting their military power before the Maltese people while so many of the islanders still lived in hovels without piped water and electricity the British had been their own worst enemy in recent years. While it was true that the British employed thousands of Maltese in the dockyards and in their colonial administration, and that the military formed the backbone of the archipelago's medical services and that the ongoing 'occupation' – if that was what it was – was essentially benign, it did little to appease the 'Malta for the Maltese' movement. Marija found the trend of nationalistic sentiments and the erosion of old loyalties very sad. Partly, this was because she knew she quite literally owed 'the British' her life but it was also because she feared what might happen if and when the Mother country abandoned 'little' Malta. There was no one political party that spoke for the whole Maltese people or even a significant proportion of them; only disparate groupings of nationalists, communists and liberals. What would happen to an archipelago of small islands in the middle of a great sea with a population of some three hundred thousand souls that was only capable of feeding a third of its people from its own resources. Malta had no oil, hardly any fresh water, and its land was arid and difficult to cultivate. Ever since the time of the Knights of St John – possibly, since the dawn of civilization – Malta had been the trading crossroads of the central Mediterranean and under the guardianship of the Royal Navy it had, Hitler's War apart, basked in what everybody understood had been a dangerously false sense of security.

The sight of the empty anchorages left Marija with a nagging feeling of loneliness, as if the soul had been hollowed out of the old world. She had grown up taking the presence of the big grey warships in the Creeks around Valletta for granted. That they were gone today was troubling; that one day they might be gone forever was...almost unthinkable.

Out of the city the country - a patchwork of fields delineated with chest high dry-stone walls - the bus picked up speed as it chugged, rattled and bounced along the pot-holed roads. The British used to trouble themselves with the potholes. Not now, why would they? They would soon be gone if, or if not gone, on their way home if the gossip and the stories in the *Times of Malta* were to be believed. It was over three years now since the Royal Naval Dockyards had been sold to a local company – Messrs C & H Bailey - and independence had seemed only a matter of time. So why bother filling the potholes in the roads?

Passing Ta'Qali airfield she half expected to see all the jet fighters and helicopters gone. Instead, two sleek shark-like fighters swooped in to land as the bus stopped at a crossroads. She was reassured to glimpse several other silvery jets parked in their blast shielded hardstands across the other side of the airfield.

Ahead, the twin cities of Mdina and Rabat stood on the rising ground overlooking Ta'Qali. As a girl she had spent endless hours on the ramparts of the hill top city gazing down on the aircraft, Spitfires, Hurricanes, twin engine Beaufighters in those seemingly long-ago days in the 1940s, taking off and landing. After the war those aircraft had been replaced with the first jet fighters; Meteors, Vampires, Hunters. She had thought their whistling, thundering engines sounded like God's fury as they climbed high in the azure blue skies over the ancient walled cities on the hill. From her bedroom window in old Rabat she awakened every morning to an eagle's eye view of the south of the island. She could see Sliema and Valletta, and sometimes if it was not too hazy the big ships manoeuvring outside Marsamxett or the entrance to the Grand Harbour. Sweeping her eye from left to right she could see the rooftops of the Three Cities – Floriana, Vittoriosa and Cospicua – across to Luqa, the flattest place on the whole Maltese Archipelago and the biggest airbase, and further west to where the fishing village of Marsaxlokk lay hidden in the morning mist. On those timeless sunny childhood mornings how could she not believe that Malta was God's own island?

The bus began to climb up the hill. At first the incline was gradual, then the road turned, twisted and soon with the increasing steepness of the gradient gears began to crash, acrid fumes began to belch from the labouring vehicle's rattling exhaust pipe. Some days the jolting, stop start bus journeys made Marija feel old and worn, today she hardly noticed, her thoughts elsewhere.

Something terrible had happened in the early hours of Sunday morning.

When the bus stopped outside the old citadel she walked at her customary measured pace towards the bridge to the medieval gate. The series of operations to straighten her left thigh and rebuild her crushed pelvis had - in a mechanical sense - worked better than even Captain Reginald Stephens – the extraordinary pioneering naval surgeon to whom she owed her life – had hoped. However, on uneven surfaces if she tried to walk too fast or forgot to consciously put one foot down, carefully, after the other, she tended to lose her balance. If she hurried overmuch, she might end up tottering like a drunk, and she was always inclined to fall harder than she ought. So, this morning, of all mornings, she walked at her own steady, relatively slow pace. There were treacherous cobblestones underfoot, testing her patience and constantly tempting her to throw out her arms like a tightrope walker.

St Catherine's Hospital for Woman was situated off the Cathedral plaza. It had opened in 1936, a jumble of small wards, treatment rooms and cupboard-sized offices in a three-storey block arranged around a cool, airy, shaded courtyard. The institution – which operated on the model of a typical small English cottage hospital catering specifically to women and children - was constantly under threat of closure; the only thing that kept it open were the tireless, indefatigable endeavours of its tigerishly formidable Chief Physician and Senior Administrative Officer, Doctor Margo Seiffert. With her nurses Margo preferred the title of 'Director' or simply 'Margo', but the authorities in Valletta tended to be more impressed by long and unnecessarily convoluted titles. Margo said it was the 'Italian streak that runs in Malta's veins.'

Marija's mother was Sicilian, her father the son of a British naval officer who had been killed in the far away Dardanelles in 1915. That she bore the surname Calleja was an accident of that sad history; her maternal grandmother having remarried in 1918 and her father assuming his step father's name. Notwithstanding her own somewhat polyglot lineage, Marija understood exactly how an outsider like Margo Seiffert could see so clearly the underlying tides in the Maltese character. Before the 1939-45 war there had been a popular movement in the Maltese Archipelago to be reunited with Italy. The war had undermined and destroyed that groundswell, possibly for many generations to come but the Maltese psyche was complex. The Phoenicians, the Greeks, the Carthaginians, the Romans, the Moors, Barbary pirates, Christian Crusaders, the Knights Hospitaller from which the Order of St John, the Knights of Malta had evolved, and latterly, the British had all been lords of Malta at one time or another – sometimes for many centuries – but each in their turn had relinquished their hold over the Maltese Archipelago; yielded to the new overlords...

The Maltese had never been their own overlords; and yet they were as a people a melange of all those peoples and religions that had ever held sway over them. Marija's father was half-British and half Maltese, her mother likewise half-Sicilian; what did that make her? A quarter of this, a half of that? And what of her parents' parents? Her mother's maternal grandparents came from Naples; her father's grandmother had been Sephardic Jew, so once upon a time – if one went back that far - Marija's distant ancestors had been expelled from Portugal in 1492. Yet she was Maltese in her soul, to the very heart of her being even if she had no idea what it actually meant to be Maltese. Would she understand herself and her heritage any better if the British left?

Marija set aside such problematic thoughts upon entering the St Catherine's Hospital for Women. The building was her second home, a second home that was with every passing day becoming her real home. Within its walls she was among her truest friends in Christendom, within a true sisterhood in which she was no longer the helpless child her parents – bless their loving souls – remembered every time they laid eyes upon her. Among her sisters Marija was her own self, free and independent and most importantly, needed.

A small crowd had gathered in the reception room on the ground floor, apparently waiting for Margo Seiffert. In the thirteen years Marija had known Margo Seiffert the sixty-one-year-old former United States Navy Surgeon-Commander had become her best friend in the world.

"Margo's been on the phone to the American Consulate in Valletta," Marija was informed in hushed tones. Margo was a small, wiry, greying bundle of restless energy who kept the clinic alive by constantly recruiting and training local nurses – nursing 'assistants', officially – from all over the archipelago.

Because of her childhood injuries from which she would never – in the eyes of officialdom – 'fully recover' Marija could never be accepted into any 'authorised' nurse training program on Malta or anywhere else. Even she had to admit, very occasionally, that she simply was not capable of performing all the duties normally expected of a nurse. However, Margo did not care about details like that. She took whatever a young woman had to offer and set about making the most of it. Inevitably, Margo had clashed with successive British Chief Medical Officers in Valletta, although not so much of late. This was yet another sign that the British were winding down what remained of their colonial administration. In fact, many of the functions of that administration had already been quietly passed, or as Margo would say 'abdicated' to local officers in recent years.

Marija had travelled to the hospital in her distinctive pale blue uniform dress. The uniform was virtually indistinguishable from that worn by junior nurses in the 'official' centrally managed infant Maltese health system, except for the absence of badges denoting her grade or place of work. St Catherine's Hospital for Women was a privately-operated institution wholly supported by gifts, donations and in no small measure the largesse of its landlord, the nearby Cathedral. Marija hung up her coat and went behind the reception desk to check the duty roster. She was pleasantly surprised to discover that she was assigned to the first floor Children's Ward that day.

Doctor Margo Seiffert bustled into the room. She took a moment to wipe the sheen of vexation off her deeply suntanned, lined face. Her once straw blond hair was grey and the gracile slenderness which would have made her figure willowy in her younger days had become sinewy, rather birdlike in her later middle age. Notwithstanding, she was exactly the same bundle of irrepressible energy whom Marija had first encountered when she had been Surgeon Captain Reginald Stephens's - the man who had patiently rebuilt her broken body - deputy and the senior orthopaedic surgical registrar at the Bighi Royal Naval Hospital at Kalkara all those years ago.

Marija had not realised until much later that the two surgeons - so utterly unalike and seemingly temperamentally utterly incompatible - had been lovers who had devoted the final years of their already brilliant careers to dragging – kicking and screaming, Malta's antiquated provisions for the health and welfare of its women and children into the twentieth century.

"Can I have your attention please!" Margo asked. Her voice was a little hoarse but as always, her manner was briskly business-like. "It feels like I've spent forever on the telephone since yesterday," she smiled ruefully, "or at least that's what it seems like!"

There was an uncomfortable mutter of amusement.

"There is good news and there is bad news," the Director of St Catherine's Hospital of Women declared. "First, the bad news. Sometime during the small hours of Sunday morning, the world went mad." She held up her hands. She planned to elaborate on her initial bald statement shortly. "The good news," she continued after the most momentary of hesitations, "is that most of the madness stopped several hundred miles to the north of us."

Margo Seiffert was already shaking her head, forestalling questions she could not possibly answer: questions that nobody could yet answer and that historians would agonise over for as long as humanity prevailed as a viable species.

"The Americans, the British and the Russians and I suspect all their allies tried to destroy each other. There's some suggestion the Russians might have attacked the Chinese. I don't know why. It doesn't matter. I'm not even sure if anybody won. All I do know is that the Russians lost. I have no idea what is left of Europe north, west or east of the Alps. I do know that Istanbul and Ankara were badly damaged in Turkey. My information is that the war is over, according to the American Embassy in Rome, anyway. When I spoke to the Consulate in Valletta the Consul told me that the British have declared martial law on Malta because they are afraid of some kind of popular rising being whipped up by communist sleeper agents. They think there may be assassinations, sabotage and quote 'Bolshevik inspired civil disobedience'. It sounded like nonsense to me but then if somebody had just dropped nuclear bombs on London, I'd be a little bit paranoid, too."

The women in the room stared dumbly, mouths agape at the older woman.

Nothing that Margo Seiffert had said had truly sunk in until then.

London bombed?

London gone?

How many people lived in London?

Six, seven million?

"I have communicated with the public health people in Valletta and offered my full support to the civilian authorities. Until I hear from them, we shall continue as normal and take what steps we can to mitigate the likely public health implications of what has happened in the north."

Marija's thoughts were jangling.

Margo was talking about fall out.

Radiation from the bombs.

"The wind is blowing from the south-east and has been blowing from that direction for the last thirty-six hours," Margo was saying. It was as if her friend and mentor was speaking to her from the far end of a long tunnel. "If and when the wind comes around to the north it will be only a matter of time before we will be threatened with fallout."

Marija listened in a daze.

Margo rarely talked about her life and career before she came to Malta. She had been married to a naval officer killed in a sea battle just before the end of the Second War. Before that war she was one of the first female surgeons in a prestigious Boston hospital, and during the 1945 war the senior orthopaedic surgeon on a hospital ship at Iwo Jima and Okinawa. The Americans had given her a row of medals for her 'bravery under fire'. After the war she had been with the American occupation forces in Berlin, Vienna, and later with the US Navy 5th Fleet Surgeon General's Staff in Naples where she had met Doctor Stephens and shortly thereafter, followed him back to Malta where Marija had first encountered her on a stiflingly hot, sultry summer day in 1949.

Margo Seiffert spoke levelly, without a trace of fear or doubt and gradually the underlying panic in the room slowly, surely subsided.

"When something terrible happens all that we can do is thank God for our blessings," the Director of the St Catherine's Hospital for Women said. "The beautiful island upon which we stand has been spared. By the grace of God, we are alive as are all our friends and our families on *this* island. Be thankful for this. Be thankful that for us life goes on and that we still have our own fate in our own hands. It is our job, our duty, to do what we can to care for the people who depend upon us now, and will come to depend upon us in the future." Suddenly, Margo clapped her hands together. "Let's get to it! We have work to do, ladies!"

Chapter 15

An extract from 'The Anatomy of Armageddon: America, Cuba, the USSR and the Global Disaster of October 1962' reproduced by the kind permission of the New Memorial University of California, Los Angeles Press published on 27th October 2012 in memoriam of the fallen.

It was not appreciated by the Kennedy White House until it was too late that 'the gallant Brits' who'd stood shoulder to shoulder with Uncle Sam in three World Wars – three wars fought, to put it crudely, to solidify American World economic and military hegemony – were never going to make the same mistake again.

Before the October War the British talked about a 'special relationship'; in Washington they talked about the benefits of having willing 'clients', a 'friends' who could be relied upon to be America's 'apologists in the councils of Europe'. True, the Brits had misbehaved back in 1956 but the Suez fiasco was in the past, and afterwards the Brits had seemed to be securely in the back pockets of the Eisenhower and Kennedy Administrations.

However, after October 1962 there was no more 'special relationship'. It is jaw-droppingly apparent from his recently published memoirs that the first post-war leader of the UKIEA – a disparate group of the survivors of Harold MacMillan's pre-war Conservative government and available members of the Labour and Liberal oppositions – Edward Heath, privately regarded the Kennedy Administration collectively as a bunch of 'freebooting murderers little better than the Nazis and on a par with the idiots in the Kremlin' who had provoked the global catastrophe. In late 1962 and early 1963 neither he, or anybody else in the world, dared say it out aloud but a terrible, unforgivable crime of unimaginable proportions had been committed and Edward Heath privately vowed, that one day there would be justice for the murdered, and for the murdered hopes of the generations to come.

In Washington, the Kennedy people were so glad they were still alive and that the USA had got away so lightly – less than five million dead and injured, between 2 and 3 percent of the population – that they honestly believed that God was on their side. As JFK toured the outskirts of the bombed cities of the north east and the deep south he talked about reconstruction, and began to build the myth of the great war of national self-preservation that the USA had been 'forced to wage' by an implacable, evil enemy who had launched an unprovoked, massive pre-meditated assault on the last best hope for civilisation. The sacred soil of the United States of America had been stained with the precious blood of its citizens, scorched by the fire of the red dragon of Marxist-Leninist evil but the American people had prevailed. America was great, its destiny never more manifest, the rightness of its cause self-evidently proven. He might have been Caesar returning from Gaul, except he was not.

In the winter of 1962-63 Kennedy and his aides were a little bewildered by the first murmurings of discontent from their surviving European allies. Initially, the Washington cabal wrote this dissonance off as a passing whimper. American charity and wisdom would make all well soon enough. This was a new age and the world was to be rebuilt in an American image. The new Romans had arrived and the world was going to be a better place in years to come.

Kennedy's people ought to have known that their 'friends' would never, ever forgive them for their hubris. The problem was that they genuinely believed they sat at God's right hand when in fact in the United Kingdom and France the survivors now viewed the Kennedy Administration as a monster kneeling obediently at the Devil's left hind claw.

If Kennedy's people had bothered to read the early assessments of their handiwork they might have repented sooner.

This is an extract from one of the first damage assessments dated 15th December 1962 and initialled by JFK on 23rd December 1962.

Strategic Air Command
Damage Assessment/United Kingdom/Serial 006412UK
Date: 12/15/62
Summary Report Status: Provisional

Command Summary

Further to Serial 0050788UK a more comprehensive damage assessment has now been carried out by teams on the ground with the cooperation of the UK Interim Emergency Administration under acting Prime Minister Heath.

The Attack

Aerial and ground surveys now confirm that twenty-three fully generated nuclear warheads detonated over or on the territory or the inshore waters of the United Kingdom.

19 (Nineteen) of these warheads were probably delivered via SS-4 or SS-5 MRBMs and four (4) by freefall bombs by Soviet Bisons which evaded the RAF fighter screen over the Norwegian Sea. Surviving RAF intercept documentation indicates that seventeen (17) of twenty-one (21) Soviet bombers were shot down short of targeting range, and the remaining hostiles were destroyed after they had made their attacks.

The attack fell mainly on London, south eastern counties and the east coast counties where US and British nuclear strike assets were located. However, there were also three strikes in the north west of England.

London. The city was hit by at least four (4) warheads in the 1-2 megaton range. All four strikes were airbursts at heights of between one thousand and three thousand feet.

Kent and Sussex. The Medway Estuary was targeted by a single 1 megaton ground burst 0.2 miles south of the dockyard complex at Chatham. Gravesend was also targeted by a single ground burst. Further airbursts targeted Manston and Canterbury.

Essex. There was a single airburst at an altitude of approximately two thousand feet one mile north of the centre of Southend.

East Anglia (including Suffolk, Norfolk and Cambridgeshire). Two (2) ground burst strikes and three (3) airburst strikes appear to have been directed at US and RAF strategic assets in the region. Both ground bursts were in relatively open countryside. One struck four miles from Mildenhall, the other six miles from Ipswich. All three airbursts detonated in the general vicinity of air bases.

Lincolnshire and Yorkshire. At least three (3) airburst strikes fell short of their intended targets detonating over coastal waters. However, one of these airbursts largely destroyed the city of Hull. Three (3) further airbursts targeted RAF V-Bomber bases. The city of Lincoln was destroyed by one airburst, and the cities of York and Leeds were severely damaged by airbursts respectively seven and six miles distant.

North West England. An airburst over the Mersey Estuary largely destroyed the city of Liverpool and its western conurbations. A second airburst approximately five miles south of Runcorn is assumed to have fallen short of either Liverpool or Barrow-in-Furness. This latter may have been the target of a third airburst seven miles to its east over Morecombe Bay. This blast caused widespread damage to Barrow and to the towns around the Bay.

Significant areas of the United Kingdom (Scotland, Wales and the Northern Ireland, the South West, West Midlands, and areas of Northern and North Eastern England) were not directly targeted and remain both economically and militarily intact. However, numerous key industrial assets have been lost, and governmental, health, and transportation infrastructures have been severely impacted. In large areas civil order has broken down and the writ

of the *UKIEA* is effective only in the
undamaged parts of the nation.

Industry and economy

Immediately after the attack industrial
production/capacity fell to approximately
10% of previous level (USA equivalent
estimate is 85%).

Within 30 days of the attack industrial
capacity had recovered to 30% (USA
equivalent is 93%).

Projected 90-day recovery estimate is
35-40% (USA 94-96%).

London and Liverpool were the two major
national dock/trading hubs and both of
these are currently dormant. However,
Southampton, Bristol and Glasgow and other
ports are gearing up to fill the gap.

A large number of air bases survived
the attack and the reestablishment of
telecommunications linkages previously
routed through London has been assigned
high priority by the UKIEA.

Disruption of power generation was
minimal but the distribution grid is
currently operating at 15% capacity
meaning large areas of the country are
subject to blackouts or have no power at
all.

Preliminary estimates are that 50% plus
of all housing stock was either destroyed
or so badly damaged as to be uninhabitable
in the current wintery conditions
prevailing across northern Europe.

Aid from around the world is only just beginning to arrive in the United Kingdom. Bottlenecks at the available ports are anticipated, and the breakdown of law and order in wide areas of the country particularly in those regions on the edge of strike zones, combined with the dislocation of the road and rail system, complicated by the early onset of winter, threatens the distribution of food and other essential supplies.

Casualty estimates

Initial estimates of between 8 and 10 million fatalities (approximately 25% of the population of England prior to the attack) now seem low.

The UKIEA now estimates deaths in the range 11 to 13 million (with perhaps 6-8 million of these deaths being from blast and burn injuries received in the attack, and other factors such as disease, exposure and the absence of normal medical facilities for the elderly, or for those who were suffering from pre-existing illnesses accounting for the higher estimates).

In undamaged areas where the UKIEA has established civil and military control death rates have stabilised. Elsewhere, best estimates are that as many as two hundred thousand (200,000) people may be dying every week from the effects of injuries received during the attack, radiation exposure, starvation, insanitary conditions, disease and starvation.

It appears that the onset of a 'nuclear winter' weather system over northern Europe is greatly adding to the difficulties of survivors. Snow has now been lying on the ground in most parts of the United Kingdom for the last seven days, during which time the temperature has not risen above 32 degrees Fahrenheit (zero degrees Celsius).

Surviving Military Capability

Ground based US Strategic Nuclear Forces: all surviving units and personnel have been airlifted out of theatre. No attempt has been made to recover inoperable Thor ICBMs which remain in situ at RAF Hemswell, Bardney, Feltwell, Coleby Grange and as many as three (3) other sites. The urgent recovery of these dual key assets has been raised with the UKIEA who have declined to prioritise the same.

Holy Loch. All SSBNs have been withdrawn from Holy Loch. Local officers of the UKIEA in the Clyde/Glasgow area have refused permission for USN support vessels and tenders to depart Holy Loch. The UKIEA has been apprised of our concerns in this regard.

RAF Strategic Nuclear Forces. Our best estimate is that a mixed force of some 30-40 serviceable V-Bombers either survived the attack or returned from missions. It is known that several V-Bombers landed away from the UK and have not yet returned to a home base. These assets have access to A-weapon stores in the UK and at surviving NATO depots under UKIEA supervision within the UK and in the Mediterranean.

RAF. Elsewhere approximately 50% of assets survive although serviceability may be low given the priority the UKIEA has given to re-establishing the strike capability of the surviving V-Bomber Force.

Army. The loss of ALL forces in Germany has impacted the morale of units in the UK. However, the surviving units in the UK are completely loyal to the UKIEA and are conducting themselves with a relatively light hand in civil policing roles in all major surviving centres of population. Units stationed overseas remain under discipline and apparently loyal to the UKIEA.

Royal Navy. Apart from the Chatham facility, none of the navy's main bases was targeted. Subsequent to the attack all units were ordered to concentrate at Plymouth, Portsmouth, Rosyth and Londonderry, or at their appropriate overseas stations. Work details from ships in UK waters were subsequently sent ashore to assist in peacekeeping and other civil emergency activities. There are no indications that major surface units overseas are being called back to home waters or redeployed to the UK's Mediterranean bases at Malta, Gibraltar and Cyprus. C-in-C UK Home Fleet has notified CINCLANT that UK Fleet movements will no longer be routinely communicated to him and that all former areas of operational co-operation are under review. The British Pacific Fleet which includes three (3) operational aircraft carriers and at least twenty other warships took no part in hostilities and was not targeted by the enemy. This force constitutes the UK's most potent remaining naval asset and is believed to be concentrating at this time on Australasian ports.

   Overall. The attack significantly degraded the UK's nuclear strike capability, eliminated up to 50% of its ground forces and its equipment, while leaving its naval forces largely intact. After the USA, the UK remains the most capable military nation on the planet.

Political Assessment

   The UKIEA is struggling to regain control of all its territory.

   The UKIEA leadership, while not openly hostile to contacts with the US Administration, clearly believes that its current situation is by and large, the fault of that Administration.

   While having requested humanitarian assistance from the USA, the UKIEA is unwilling at this time to discuss military co-operation of any kind, or future European reconstruction plans with the USA.

The leader of the UKIEA has communicated his dissatisfaction and extreme disappointment with the quantity and the quality of the USA's assistance thus far, to the UK, and to the relatively undamaged departments of western and southern France.

The leader of the UKIEA has further cautioned the USA not to see the current situation as an invitation to 'interfere in the affairs of the Mediterranean'.

There are reports (unconfirmed) that the British Pacific Fleet, including the fleet carrier Ark Royal, may be planning to redeploy to the Persian Gulf, presumably to safeguard oil supplies in the event US help is not forthcoming.

US vessels have been refused permission to dock at Gibraltar and at Malta in the last seven days with port authorities citing the need to prioritise 'emergency support operations' over hosting 'inappropriate courtesy visits by foreign vessels.'

British troops are now guarding CENTO's Cyprus stockpile of 40 fully generated nuclear warheads, having previously removed all US personnel from the base outside Larnica.

There are suggestions from Intelligence sources that there may be a growing *disconnect between the UKIEA leadership and its military high command.*

This blasé, and largely misleading assertion in the last paragraph, which had been allowed to pass unchallenged by the State Department, the Pentagon, the CIA and the National Security Council before it got into JFK's hands is symptomatic of the mood of the times.

The inhabitants of JFK's by then lightly radioactive modern Camelot – allegedly the 'best and the brightest' of their generation – had blundered into an unnecessary war and allowed Curtis LeMay, the gung-ho Chief of Staff of the US Air Force, to run amok. The 'best and the brightest' had betrayed not just their own generation, but generations to come. The 'best and the brightest', having presided over the massacre of their European Allies were already, in the winter of 1962-63 too preoccupied wringing their hands and attempting to justify their folly to pause to read the runes of the future. They thought they had inherited one world from the ashes of the old, instead they had inherited another in which they would be friendless pariahs for all their military might, economic effulgence and ultimately, selfish and futile, good intentions.

In the months after the October War the Kennedy White House had the opportunity to become the saviour of western civilization. In the event it fluffed its lines, opted for parsimony and in the end sowed the seeds for new conflicts.

There were some in Washington – not many but some – who cautioned against the post-war tide of national rebirth; but nobody in the White House was listening.

However, not even the most pessimistic of Kennedy's critics anticipated that things could go wrong so quickly. America enjoyed a year of dominion, the mistress of all it surveyed without comprehending that it was the master of nothing.

And then the unthinkable happened.

The next war.

Chapter 16

08:44 Hours Zulu
Monday 29th October 1962
HMS Dreadnought, Barrow-in-Furness

Lieutenant-Commander Simon Collingwood read his orders one last time and with a sigh and a sinking feeling in the pit of his stomach he concluded that he had no alternative but to obey them. Flag Officer Submarines was alive and if not exactly on top form, ensconced in a bunker at Devonport Naval Dockyard and his word was law.

There was a knock at the door.

Simon Collingwood turned the two sheets of paper he had been staring at upside down on the blotter of his narrow desk.

"Yes!"

Lieutenant Dick Manville stuck his head around the door jam.

"The Chief reports he has taken charge of the Emergency War Supplies Store, sir."

"Any trouble?"

"No, sir. The guards were nowhere to be seen and none of the civilians roaming around the base had attempted to break in. The Chief has posted armed men and he's gathering up odds and sods for a proper guard detail."

The Acting Captain of HMS Dreadnought was exhausted but he did not have time to be tired, let alone to snatch a few hours' sleep. He felt like he had been in constant motion ever since he was roused out of his bed over thirty hours ago. He stifled a groan, knowing he could not afford to show his weariness even in front of a decent fellow like Dick Manville.

"What about the priority inventory items we need?"

"All present and correct. Unfortunately, there is no reserve for issue to the civilian authorities. There will be Hell to pay when the civvies find out, sir."

Overnight another forty-one naval personnel had reported to Dreadnought. About half these men had been attached to the new Tribal class frigate Mowhawk, fitting out in a nearby dock, others were technicians assigned to the yard, and the remainder either lived in the area or had come to Barrow to report in simply because it was the nearest appropriate base.

Collingwood had sent out a party to secure the local Territorial Army barracks and to seize any weapons it found. He had surprised himself how quickly he had begun to make hard decisions. At first, he hoped to be able to combine the operational imperative of securing the immediate area around Dreadnought with safeguarding his civilian charges, but he privately accepted before he had received orders from Fleet Command that this was not going to be possible.

Most of the civilian dockyard workers had melted away and none of the senior managers had come into the yard since the attack. Simon Collingwood had found himself in command of not only his uncompleted submarine but of the entire dockyard complex. He had received requests for men to help put out the fires in the town, rescue people trapped in collapsed houses and to provide backup for the virtually non-existent medical services. With insufficient men to secure the dockyard he had to refuse all pleas for assistance.

Collingwood hardened his heart anew. In the new world in which they lived today's hard decisions would be the first of many to come in the days, weeks and years to come. His people, his ship came first. Even if Dreadnought had not been the most sophisticated and the most powerful vessel in the Fleet, even if she had just been a worn-out old minesweeper, she would have come first. Once he reminded himself of his duty his thoughts had swiftly clarified and his resolve set in concrete.

Radioactive fallout was the problem.

Dreadnought could not be made fit for sea for some weeks so she could not steam out into the North Channel and sit out the worst of the radioactive bloom from the attack underwater. Nor could she batten down in the graving dock. She had no internal power and was totally reliant on the land for succour. Therefore, her people, *his* people *had* to be protected as best as possible while the boat was being made ready for sea.

Simon Collingwood the man, wanted to protect the civilians sheltering on board HMS Dreadnought; Lieutenant-Commander Simon Collingwood, the acting Commanding Officer of Britain's first and only nuclear-powered submarine did not have a remit for sentimentality. In a universe in which the average temperature was approximately two degrees above absolute zero there were, inevitably, times when the well of pity ran dry and this was one such time.

The acting-Captain of HMS Dreadnought redrew his immediate priorities.

One – secure the boat.

Two – draft men with technical or operational experience and, or expertise onto the boat's roster.

Three – activate the boat's Westinghouse S5W reactor.

Four – the boat would join 1st Submarine Squadron at Devonport to prepare for her first operational deployment at the earliest date.

Simon Collingwood turned his mind to practicalities.

Securing the boat and identifying men with critical skills would be a relatively straightforward business. Activating the boat's reactor would be fraught with dangers. Sailing the boat to Devonport was something he would worry about if he survived reactor activation.

First things first.

In the training and preparation of its first nuclear submariners, the Royal Navy had adopted the tried and tested US Navy model. Simon Collingwood's training had been long, arduous and comprehensive. He knew Dreadnought's systems from bow to stern and from the keel to the top of her fin-like sail. Most of all he was a highly qualified reactor engineer fully conversant with the protocols of safe operation and more importantly, all the things that could go wrong with a nuclear power plant. Moreover, he had medical practitioner's understanding of radioactive contamination and its effect on the human body.

The radiation monitor he had had mounted in the cockpit at the top of the sail had not gone off the scale *yet*. Notwithstanding, all protective and prophylactic measures against fallout products needed to be instituted *now*.

Fallout was likely to contain three specific isotopic threats: strontium-90, iodine-131 and 133. Some warheads were intrinsically 'dirtier' than others and Soviet weapons tended to be 'dirtier' than their western counterparts. However, there was no point worrying about that because there was very little anybody could do to mitigate against the effects of irradiation by the majority of the more esoteric and short-lived fusion and, or fission isotopic by-products. The main thing was to focus on the longer-lived killers that one knew *had* to be constituent parts of *any* fallout cloud.

The physics of nuclear fallout both terrified and oddly, reassured Simon Collingwood as he organised his thoughts and regimented his emotions to do what he must do in the next minutes, hours, days and months. The situation was so desperate that only in duty was there a semblance of peace of mind.

The most dangerous fallout by product of a nuclear explosion was strontium-90. Sr90 is a *bone seeker* which biochemically behaves like calcium the next lightest of the *group 2 elements*. Like calcium, after ingestion about 70–80% of the dose gets excreted but virtually all remaining Sr90 is deposited in bone and bone marrow. About 1% of the total dose accumulates in blood and soft tissue. The presence of relatively low concentrations of Sr90 in bones greatly increases the risk of developing bone cancer, cancers in adjacent soft tissue or leukaemia. The biological half-life of Sr90 in the human body was approximately eighteen years. Sr90 attacks the bone marrow and destroys the body's ability to produce the white blood cells necessary to fight infection. Anybody breathing in air, or consuming food or fluids heavily contaminated by Sr90 might die of something as innocent as the common cold within a week.

It was known that calcium citrate helped the body resist Sr90 by competing with Sr90. This works because bone and bone marrow can only absorb isotopic contaminants at a given rate. Calcium citrate will therefore, reduce Sr90 take up and therefore reduce the total level of contamination. The recommended dosage of calcium citrate was 1000 milligrams daily – adults and children – immediately after an attack, and thereafter 500 milligrams per day for three weeks. In addition to calcium citrate prophylactic doses of vitamin C (ascorbic acid) tended to regulate the production of bone protein and promote the formation of white blood cells. The recommended dosage of Vitamin C was 300 milligrams a day for a month after the first fallout and 100 milligrams daily thereafter for least two months.

After Sr90 the next most dangerous fallout isotopes were iodine131 and iodine133. Radioactive I131 and I133 iodine collects in the thyroid gland in the neck. Adults exposed to these radioactive isotopes of iodine acquire a massively heightened risk of cancer; and because the thyroid gland regulates growth children exposed to these isotopes are likely to be stunted and prone to childhood cancers. It was known that potassium iodide – a daily dose of 130 milligrams taken for at least the first hundred days after an attack - helped to inhibit the build-up of I131 and I133 in the thyroid.

Lieutenant-Commander Simon Collingwood completed his brief, didactic review of the situation. He knew exactly what needed to be done and there was nothing to be gained by delaying or attempting in any way, shape or form to finesse the brutality of the decision he was about to make.

Dreadnought's store of potassium iodide, calcium citrate and vitamin C tablets was sufficient to provide a minimal level of fallout protection to the men he needed to get the boat to sea. He had no surplus to spare for useless hands.

His orders were unambiguous.

'HMS Dreadnought will make ready for sea with all urgency. CO HMS Dreadnought is hereby empowered to take any measures appropriate to requisition staff and resources to achieve this outcome at the earliest date. Lethal force is hereby authorised against any person, military or civilian who obstructs CO Dreadnought and or, any of his personnel in this work. CO Dreadnought is expressly forbidden to divert resources at his disposal to civilian defence or relief operations....'

Welcome to the brave new world!

The Commanding Officer of HMS Dreadnought cleared his throat.

"We must clear the boat of civilians," he said resignedly as he rose to his feet and jammed his cap on his head.

Chapter 17

10:15 Hours Zulu
Monday 29th October 1962
HMS Talavera, 88 Miles East of Whitby

Lieutenant Peter Christopher shut the door of his claustrophobic cabin beneath the bridge and drew up the chair in front of the small, sharp edged plywood counter that served as his desk. His bunk took up most of the rest of the space in the compartment. Hard-edged overhead lockers threatened to brain him if he moved his long, angular frame without extreme due care and attention in any direction.

Talavera was riding relatively easily on her anchors, her bow pointed into the wind and the serried ranks of eight to ten-foot waves. Every now and then one of the screws churned and the anchor capstans rattled as the destroyer adjusted her heading. The wind was slipping around to the south and nobody knew if that was a good or a bad thing. As if it mattered. Fallout would be everywhere in time.

Peter was officially off watch but the Old Man had ordered him to take a break on his last round of the ship. No man on board had conducted himself more calmly than Commander David Penberthy. He had regularly addressed the crew over the tannoy, and every ninety minutes or so he strolled from stem to stern, patting men on the back, his affable manner and his unruffled presence suggesting that whatever anybody else believed, that not all was lost. His had been an object lesson in grace under pressure.

"You don't have to try to put your head down, Peter," the Captain had said, paternally. "I don't think any of us can do that right now. Just have a few moments to yourself. Stretch your legs. Look in on the wardroom. Have a stiff drink. I need my officers to keep their heads on their shoulders. You can't take care of your department if you're not taking care of yourself."

Peter Christopher had looked into the Wardroom.

Drunk over-stewed coffee.

He had chatted with the Executive Officer, Hugo Montgommery, who had just completed his own walk around the ship. Back in his cabin Peter had pulled out a pad of writing paper and begun to write.

Dear Marija,

I don't know if you will ever receive this letter. I hope with all my heart that you do receive it because then at least, I will know that you have come through today's madness. I'm not a religious fellow – as I think you know! – but if I was, I'd be praying for you and your family and friends. I don't know if Malta has escaped the fire but if it has then perhaps there is a God after all.

Rather more by luck than anything else, I suspect, we on Talavera have survived. We were well out at sea running radar trials when the balloon went up. Presently, we are riding on our forward anchors in a hundred feet of water on top of the Dogger Bank out in the middle of the North Sea.

The Captain is a seaman of the old school and when the madness began, he pointed us out to sea and kept on going for as long as there was fuel in the bunkers. Running away was all we could do. Our magazines are empty, a third of our crew hasn't come aboard yet and we're two or three months away from being anywhere near operational. So, anyway, here we are riding on our anchors in the middle of a south westerly gale.

We're detecting the first fallout clouds but we're pretty well sealed up and the sick bay took on a full ABC inventory before we sailed. We've got enough iodine and calcium citrate tablets to see us through the next six weeks, apparently. Because Talavera is virtually a new build, we've got brand new filters in the ventilation ducts and all the hatches are dogged down as tight as you like. What with one thing and another we're sitting as pretty as we could possibly have hoped. We've got enough rations on board – if we stretch them out - to stay at sea ten or eleven days. The only fly in the ointment is that we're low on bunker oil. We'll be able to keep power in the ship, pump the bilges and manoeuvre if we have to but it'll be touch and go if we can make port if we stay out here more than a few days.

Morale on board is fairly good, probably because the chaps haven't had much chance to stop to think. The Captain has had us busy closing up the ship, drilling and checking equipment all day. I think the worst thing is not really knowing what's happened back on land.

The Captain has broadcast that London and targets in East Anglia and further up the East Coast of England have been hit. More than that we don't know. The only people on the ship who saw anything at all were fellows on the bridge. They reported the night being turned into day several times and a sort of 'lightning effect' over the western horizon. The main attack lasted about an hour. After that there were a handful of big flashes in the sky between three and four o'clock, and nothing since. We'd turned off most of our radio and radar kit at that stage in case it got damaged but I don't think it made any difference. We've got equipment failures in several systems because the cack-handed way the yard wired everything it was virtually impossible to tell what had power in it and what didn't until it was too late. Hopefully, tracing the failures will keep my people busy and stop them worrying about things they can't do anything about.

The good news is that we've received broadcasts from Fleet HQ in the last couple of hours and picked up radio traffic from other ships so we know we're not alone out here.

An hour ago, we received the 'cease hostilities' order. I don't know if it means the war is over. I hope it is over although Talavera is still closed up at Condition Two (that's one step below battle stations).

Peter Christopher hesitated, waves of weariness sweeping over him like the grey, spume flecked swells sweeping under Talavera's sharp prow. He pulled open the drawer beneath the desk, withdrew the three small framed photographs. He turned them over, stared.

The first small photograph was of his father, his mother and his sister on the day he passed out of Dartmouth. Eight years ago, it might have been in another lifetime. His mother had died five years ago, a mercy in the circumstances. His sister had married an engineer and emigrated to Australia in 1958. As for the Admiral? Peter had not had much to do with his father since his mother had died. The Admiral was a stranger. He had recently gone out to the Far East to take command of the Pacific Fleet; Peter had read about the appointment in the Navy Gazette. Even on that day eight years ago in the sunshine at Dartmouth the Admiral had been inscrutable, his expression at odds with the smiles of his mother and sister

'The Christophers graduate at the top of their classes,' the hero of those long-ago Malta convoys, and the former implacable U-boat hunting commander of an elite Western Approaches escort groups had observed. '*Not* half-way down the list.'

The Admiral had seemed miffed that he had opted to let the Navy send him back to University. The Christophers were seagoing, fighting sailors not 'technicians and staff flunkies.' People assumed the Admiral routinely pulled strings to oil his progress from one plum posting to another; nothing could be further from the truth. Peter might have been disowned for all he knew.

Marija was the only person in whom he had ever confided how much his father's estrangement and his coldly distant disappointment had hurt him as a boy, and continued to wound him even now. His mother's premature death at fifty-three, hastened by loneliness and drink, had sharpened the edge of his pain and anger and made the breach with his father almost irreconcilable.

The second picture was of the Calleja siblings. He gazed at the faded monochrome portrait of Marija aged fourteen, her elder brother Sam, and younger brother Joe on a balcony with the Grand Harbour at their backs. Sam, four years older, obviously felt he was too old for such nonsense as family snaps. Joe would have been only ten or eleven at the time, and Marija – having temporarily put aside her crutches - had her arms around Sam's waist and Joe's shoulders. Sam was half-frowning, Joe was grinning guiltily and Marija was laughing, her long dark hair catching on the light summer breeze.

The Admiral had commanded a cruiser squadron based at Malta at the time and Peter's mother – having deposited him and his sister, Elspeth in boarding schools in England – had gone out to join the hero in Valletta for the last six months of his first seagoing posting as a newly promoted Rear-Admiral. In Malta, his mother, as was her way, had enthusiastically thrown herself into the social whirl of the Mediterranean Fleet, and devoted much of her spare time to miscellaneous good causes. Malta had been wrecked by bombing during the war and in the cash-strapped years of the late forties' reconstruction was painfully slow. Thousands of Maltese were still living among the ruins and basic services like water supply, electricity, and hospitals were operating at a level that would never have been tolerated in England.

It was during the course of his mother's 'good works' that she encountered the Calleja family, and their 'crippled' daughter, Marija whom, along with her baby brother Joe had been miraculously rescued from their collapsed home in Vittoriosa twenty-four hours after a German air raid in 1942. There had been few such miracles during the Malta blitz and even in 1950 Marija's story still attracted a great deal of local interest. At the time Peter Christopher's mother had encountered the Calleja family, Marija had been in a year-long interregnum between a series of major operations that a remarkable naval surgeon called, Reginald Stephens hoped would eventually enable the 'Heroine of Vittoriosa-Birgu' to one day, walk again unaided by crutches or sticks.

While Peter Christopher's mother had been unable to offer any real additional practical support - the medical side of things was already well in hand – she had been captivated by the vivacious, laughing girl child in the wheelchair. In retrospect Peter suspected that those few months in Malta were among the happiest of his mother's life. She had become tremendously friendly with Marija's mother, an unlikely friendship given that she was the daughter of English country gentlefolk and Marija Calleja, the proud descendent of honest Sicilian peasant farmers. The two women had corresponded until his mother's death, never so far as he knew confiding each other's secrets to another living soul. Peter's mother had been completely captivated by Marija and it had been a terrible wrench for her to leave Malta. Back in England she was a changed woman, aware for the first time how 'shamelessly' – her own word – she had been 'neglecting' her own children. Practically her last act before leaving Malta was to ask Marija if she would consider writing to a pen friend in England. At the time she had had in mind Elspeth, Peter's elder sister. Elspeth had been mortally offended by the notion of having a pen friend several years her junior – Elspeth was then nearly sixteen and Marija just eleven - and in any event, that sort of thing was not her cup of tea. So it was that Peter had become the heroine of Vittoriosa-Birgu's English pen friend.

That was more than half his life ago.

The pen friends latest exchange of portraits had been that spring.

Peter gazed at the image that seized his whole attention every time he trusted himself to look upon it. Marija had sent him the specially posed, studio head and shoulders monochrome picture, six inches by four, which he had had mounted in a silvery frame in Edinburgh. There was a small crucifix on a slender chain hanging from her neck. Her skin was clean and clear, her eyes focused a little off camera to show her face in half profile. Her hair was pulled back in a traditional, and to modern eyes, almost Edwardian way and her expression was intent rather than serious, her eyes were smiling...

It is odd that as I write everything around me on the ship seems so normal. Everybody is going about their duties and the ship is quiet, just like it was a normal first watch. I don't think what has happened has really begun to sink in yet.

Peter had been engaged once – last year to a vicar's daughter called Phoebe – but it would never have worked. On the face of it, Phoebe was very nearly the perfect wife for a career naval officer; petite, clever, pragmatic and devout, she believed in service and in the virtue of duty, and she had latched onto him like a limpet. He had been flattered, mildly infatuated with her for several months and not realised the error of his ways until he found himself *engaged*; although he could not later actually remember ever uttering the fateful question: 'Will you, Phoebe Louise Sellars, do me, the honour of marrying me?" However, Phoebe was far too well brought up a young lady to have lied a about a thing like that and it would have been extremely bad form to have disputed her word on such a sensitive matter. Especially, after Phoebe's father had had the engagement announced in *The Times*. One day they were 'dating', the next Phoebe was discussing the seating plan for the wedding reception.

It had taken him over a fortnight – three or four letters - before he dared confess his 'problem' to Marija, and another week before she replied, by airmail. Customarily their letters went by overland mail or by the normal shipping routes and sometimes took weeks to arrive. Strangely, when he was based at Simon's Town near the southern tip of Africa his letters had invariably reached Malta within the week, whereas, from England there was no telling when Marija would receive his latest missive, or he would receive her latest news. Sometimes, letters mysteriously arrived out of sequence so they had got into the habit of appending a footnote to each letter specifying to which communication they were replying.

Marija had not been upset, or jealous, or angry in any way with his foolishness. She' knew from his previous correspondence on the subject that he had not, by any stretch of the imagination, fallen in love with Phoebe Sellars and did not think their 'relations' would survive his next sea going posting.

"Have you told her about me?" Marija had asked rhetorically.

He had once, innocently in passing, and Phoebe had been rather stuffy about it so he had not mentioned it again.

"You and I tell each other everything," Marija's letter had reminded him. "If I was your wife, I would not put up with it. I would insist that you stopped writing to that brazen Mediterranean temptress! Three is company, as you English say!"

He had known Marija was being tongue-in-cheek but nevertheless he had been struck by the fact she was not mincing her words. It was as if she understood how torn he was to be considering breaking – he had been ever since the reality of the 'engagement' had sunk in - with Phoebe. He was not, and had never been, a choirboy, notwithstanding he tended, rather clumsily and guiltily, glossed over his easy come easy go affairs with girlfriends and other women in his letters. He had not known what Marija had read between the lines over the years, or even if she had strong views on the subject. Not until *that* letter.

'If I was your wife, I would not put up with it...'

Marija had never mentioned a boyfriend of her own. Marija was lively, articulate, funny, beautiful and the Maltese valued marriage and family above practically all things so he had always assumed that one day she would write to him to inform him of her own forthcoming nuptials.

Three is company, as you English say!

That letter had turned everything he had taken for granted about his *pen friend's* feelings for him on their head.

"There are only three things you can do," Marija had counselled. "Firstly, you must marry her. She sounds like a very nice and very well brought up young woman who plans to support you in your career and will almost certainly fill up your home with bambinos. Secondly, you can tell her that you don't love her and that your engagement is over. This would be cruel and she would spend the rest of her life wondering why you could not find it in your heart to love her, and how she could have misjudged a rascal like you so badly."

Peter Christopher had smiled as he read these words, reassured before he read, and re-read, a dozen or twenty times, the following lines.

"Thirdly," Marija had advised him, "you must never write to me again."

Fortuitously, Phoebe had broken off the engagement a few days later.

If he stopped writing to Marija a part of him, possibly, the best part of him would have withered and died. He would literally, have rather cut off his right arm than lose Marija for if he had a soul mate in this world it was Marija Elizabeth Calleja.

The breach with Phoebe had been about this time last year and he had become a monastic figure in the months since. Then, just before they sailed from Chatham the confirmation news had come through that in March next year Talavera was to relieve her sister ship, HMS Agincourt, and commence a two-year attachment to the 7th Destroyer Squadron in Malta.

Peter had not had time to dash off a letter to Marija with the good news before they sailed. March was still a long way off and there would be plenty of time to compose a *proper*, serious and suitably restrained epistle communicating the future movements of Her Majesty's Ship Talavera. Three days ago, there had seemed to be all the time in the world. All the time in the world to contemplate the depth and the true nature of his feelings for the woman whom he had never met but to whom he felt inextricably linked.

And then the world had gone mad.

Malta was Headquarters of the Mediterranean Fleet, a prime target for Soviet medium range ballistic missiles in Bulgaria and the Balkans, and nuclear bombers based in the Ukraine and the Crimea. Even now Malta might be a scorched radioactive desert, uninhabitable for generations.

No, no, no...

However, it seems to me that no matter how bad things are we cannot afford to give in. If we despair then we are lost. While we survive, while Talavera and my crewmates survive, we owe it to ourselves to be worthy of surviving.

Everything has changed but some things remain the same. You have always been and will always remain my best friend in the world and the one person I trust above all others. As I write I am looking at your picture. While I look at your face, I can still believe that there is hope.

If we both live please wait for me because I am on my way to you.

[The End]

Author's Endnote

'Operation Anadyr' is Book 1 of the alternative history series *Timeline 10/27/62*.

Why *Timeline 10/27/62?* Because that date is a very significant date in my life and in the lives of everybody else in the world alive today because on Saturday 27th October 1962 World War III *almost* started. World War III probably would not have lasted very long because one side would have been swiftly obliterated in the first 24 hours of a cataclysm that would have left vast tracts of the Northern Hemisphere uninhabited and uninhabitable for decades to come. Perhaps, a quarter of the world's population would have died in the firestorm or in the starvation and the plagues that would have ensued in the following weeks and months.

In the October War of 1962 the hammer of the gods would have fallen upon the territories of the Soviet Union, central and Western Europe, and to a lesser extent, upon the extremities of continental North America. In the Soviet Union and in Europe from Paris to Warsaw, from Prague to Berlin, from the Alps to the Baltic, across the Low Countries and parts of the United Kingdom the thermonuclear fire would have burned with a merciless flame. Scandinavia might have escaped relatively untouched, likewise southern France, Italy, Spain and Portugal, Ireland and possibly parts of England, Wales and Scotland.

The 'Cuban Missiles' War would have been a Man-made global catastrophe like no other in human history. In the aftermath, the USA, mourning the dead in half-a-dozen wrecked cities would have been the last major industrial and military power left standing. That world could never, ever be the world we know today.

How close did we actually come to the edge of the abyss? Much closer than most people like to contemplate. On Saturday 27th October 1962, north east of Cuba, the commander of Soviet submarine B-59 had to be talked out of firing a nuclear-tipped torpedo at the American destroyer USS Beale. *That's how close we came to World War III!*

The Captain of the B-59 was a man called Valentin Grigorievitch Savitsky. He was exhausted, the air in his vessel was virtually unbreathable and he was at the end of his tether. He may have believed that war had already broken out between the USSR and America. In any event he gave the order for a nuclear warhead to be fitted to a torpedo.

Allegedly he said: *"We're going to blast them now! We will die, but we will sink them all! We will not disgrace our Navy!"* From which we may infer that he was in earnest.

In that era Soviet naval doctrine governing the deployment of tactical nuclear weapons on board a warship at sea required the authorisation of three officers: the captain, the executive officer, and the vessel's political officer. B-59's political officer, Ivan Semonovich Maslennikov signed off on starting World War III but fortunately for us all, the submarine's second-in-command, Captain 2nd Rank Vasili Arkhipov, dissented and Armageddon was narrowly averted.

Timeline 10/27/62 is an alternative history of the modern world in which nobody ever got to know the name of Vasili Arkhipov because he died in the first act of the most terrible war in history.

Operation Anadyr is the first verse in the story of what happened after Vasili Arkhipov failed to prevail upon Valentin Grigorievitch Savitsky to see reason.

To the reader: firstly, thank you for reading this book; and secondly, please remember that this is a work of fiction. I made it up in my own head. None of the characters in *'Operation Anadyr – Book 1 of the 'Timeline 10/27/62 Series'* - is based on real people I know of, or have ever met. Nor do the specific events described in *'Operation Anadyr'* - *Book 1 of the 'Timeline 10/27/62 Series'* - have, to my knowledge, any basis in real events I know to have taken place. Any resemblance to real life people or events is, therefore, unintended and entirely coincidental.

The *'Timeline 10/27/62 Series'* is an alternative history of the modern world and because of this, real historical characters are referenced and in some cases their words and actions form significant parts of the narrative. I have no way of knowing for sure if these real, historical figures, would have spoken thus, or acted in the ways I depict them acting. Any word I place in the mouth of a real historical figure, and any action which I attribute to them after 27th October 1962 *never* actually happened. As I always say in my Author's Notes to my readers, *I made it up in my own head.*

A brief note on ships and ship names and the old counties of England: HMS Talavera (*Yard no. 617*) was a later Battle Class destroyer laid down at John Brown and Company's Yard on the Clyde on 29th August 1944 and launched, on 27th August 1945 to clear the slip. The hull was sold to the West of Scotland Shipbreaking Company Limited of Troon, in South Ayrshire, where it was beached on 26th January 1946. Breaking up commenced on 5th February 1946 and was completed on 27th March 1946.

Four of HMS Talavera's younger sisters - Agincourt, Aisne, Barossa and Corunna – were converted to Fast Air Detection Escorts and all served, at one time or another, with the Mediterranean Fleet and were once based at Malta. Their conversions were interim, stop gap measures which were overtaken by events. First, Harold Wilson's Labour Government cancelled the new big fleet carriers they were supposed to be escorting; and secondly, new technology and new ships soon rendered them obsolete. All four Fast Air Detection Battles were decommissioned before the end of the

1960s in a universe in which HMS Talavera never steamed.

HMS Dreadnought was the United Kingdom's first nuclear powered hunter killer submarine. On 27th October 1962, Dreadnought was fitting out at Barrow-in-Furness.

Barrow-in-Furness now sits – since 1974 - in the English county of *Cumbria*; in October 1962 prior to a major reorganisation of English local government the Furness Peninsula was still in the northern part of *Lancashire.*

As with real historical characters, real historical ships are treated in a documentary - where they were and as they were deployed - fashion up to and including 27th October 1962. Thereafter, all bets are off because in this post cataclysm timeline, *everything changes.*

Thank you again for reading *Timeline 10/27/62 – Book 1: Operation Anadyr.* I hope you enjoyed it - or if you didn't, sorry - but either way, thank you for reading and helping to keep the printed word alive. Remember, civilisation depends on people like *you.*

'Operation Anadyr' was deliberately conceived as a novella to offer readers a relatively short 'game book', or starting point for the *Timeline 10/27/62 Series*; this is what happened, some reasons why, and this is the world we are now living in. Starting with *'Love is Strange'* Book 2 in series jumps into

the Timeline 10/27/62 World and begins telling the story of what happened *after Armageddon*.

As a rule, I let my books speak for themselves. I hope it does not sound fuddy-duddy or old-fashioned, but broadly speaking I tend towards the view that a book *should* speak for itself.

However, with your indulgence I would like briefly – well, as briefly as is possible without being overly terse – to share a few personal thoughts with you, the reader about the *Timeline 10/27/62 World*.

I was not yet seven-and-a-half years old in October 1962 when I realised my parents were paying an awful lot of attention to the radio, devouring every line of print in their daily newspaper and were not quite themselves, a little distracted in fact, now that I think about it. I heard the word 'Cuba' bandied about but did not know until much later that the most dangerous moment of my life had come and gone without my ever, as a child, knowing it.

I was not yet eight-and-a-half years old when one day in November 1963 the World around me came, momentarily, to a juddering halt. I had heard the name of John Fitzgerald Kennedy, and I even knew that he was the President of something called the United States of America. I did not know then that he was a womanising, drug dependent and deeply conflicted man who had lied to the American people about his chronic, periodically disabling illness which in any rational age ought to have disqualified him from the Presidency; *but I did know that he was a charismatic, talismanic figure in whom even I, as a child more interested in soccer, model trains and riding my new bicycle, had invested a nameless hope for the future.* And then one day he was gone and I shared my parents' shock and horror. It was not as if a mortal man had been murdered; JFK had become a mythic figure long before then. It was as if the modern-day analogue of King Menelaus of Sparta - hero of the Trojan Wars and the husband of Helen, she of the legendary face that launched a thousand ships - had been gunned down that day in Dallas.

The Cuban Missiles crisis and the death of a President taught a young boy in England in 1962 and 1963 that the World is a very dangerous place.

Many years later we learned how close we all came to the abyss in late October 1962. Often, we look back on how deeply Jack Kennedy's death scarred hearts and minds in the years after his assassination.

There is no certainty, no one profound insight into what 'might have happened' had the Cold War turned *Hot* in the fall of 1962, or if JFK had survived that day in Dallas. History is not a systematic, explicable march from one event to another that inevitably reaches some readily predictable outcome. History only works that way in hindsight; very little is *obvious* either to the major or the minor players *at the time* history is actually being made. Nor does one have to be a fully paid up chaos theoretician to know that apparently inconsequential events can have massive unforeseen and unforeseeable impacts in subsequent historical developments.

I do not pretend to *know* what would have happened if the USA and the USSR had gone to war over Cuba in October 1962. One imagines this scenario has been the object of countless staff college war games in America and elsewhere in the intervening fifty-three years; I suspect – with a high level of confidence - that few of those war games would have played out the way the participants expected, and that no two *games* would have resolved themselves in exactly the same way as any other. That is the beauty and the fascination of historical counterfactuals, or as those of us who make no pretence at being emeritus professors of history say, *alternative history*.

Nobody can claim 'this is the way it would have been' after the Cuban Missiles Crisis 'went wrong'. This author only *speculates* that the Timeline 10/27/62 Series reflects one of the many ways 'things might have gone' in the aftermath of Armageddon.

The only thing one can be reasonably confident about is that if the Cuban Missiles Crisis had turned into a shooting war the World in which we live today would, *probably*, not be the one with which we are familiar.

A work of fiction is a journey of imagination. I hope it does not sound corny but I am genuinely a little humbled by the number of people who have already bought into what I am trying to do with *Timeline 10/27/62.*

Like any author, this author would prefer everybody to enjoy his books – if I disappoint, I am truly sorry – but either way, thank you for reading and helping to keep the printed word alive. I really do believe that civilization depends on people like *you.*

Other Books by James Philip

New England Series

Book 1: Empire Day
Book 2: Two Hundred Lost Years
Book 3: Travels Through the Wind
Book 4: Remember Brave Achilles
Book 5: George Washington's Ghost

Coming in 2020

Book 6: The Imperial Crisis

River Hall Chronicles

Book 1: Things Can Only get Better
Book 2: Consenting Adults
Book 3: All Swing Together

Coming in 2020

Book 4: The Honourable Member

The Guy Winter Mysteries
Prologue: Winter's Pearl
Book 1: Winter's War
Book 2: Winter's Revenge
Book 3: Winter's Exile
Book 4: Winter's Return
Book 5: Winter's Spy
Book 6: Winter's Nemesis

The Bomber War Series
Book 1: Until the Night
Book 2: The Painter
Book 3: The Cloud Walkers

Until the Night Series
Part 1: Main Force Country – September 1943
Part 2: The Road to Berlin – October 1943
Part 3: The Big City – November 1943
Part 4: When Winter Comes – December 1943
Part 5: After Midnight – January 1944

The Harry Waters Series
Book 1: Islands of No Return
Book 2: Heroes
Book 3: Brothers in Arms

The Frankie Ransom Series
Book 1: A Ransom for Two Roses
Book 2: The Plains of Waterloo
Book 3: The Nantucket Sleighride

The Strangers Bureau Series
Book 1: Interlopers
Book 2: Pictures of Lily

James Philip's Cricket Books

F.S. Jackson
Lord Hawke

Audio Books of the following Titles
are available (or are in production) now

Aftermath
After Midnight
A Ransom for Two Roses
Brothers in Arms
California Dreaming
Empire Day
Heroes
Islands of No Return
Love is Strange
Main Force Country
Operation Anadyr
Red Dawn
The Big City
The Cloud Walkers
The Nantucket Sleighride
The Painter
The Pillars of Hercules
The Plains of Waterloo
The Road to Berlin
Travels Through the Wind
Two Hundred Lost Years
Until the Night
When Winter Comes
Winter's Exile
Winter's Pearl
Winter's Return
Winter's Revenge
Winter's Spy
Winter's War

Cricket Books edited by James Philip

The James D. Coldham Series
[Edited by James Philip]

Books

Northamptonshire Cricket: A History [1741-1958]
Lord Harris

Anthologies

Volume 1: Notes & Articles
Volume 2: Monographs No. 1 to 8

Monographs

No. 1 - William Brockwell
No. 2 - German Cricket
No. 3 - Devon Cricket
No. 4 - R.S. Holmes
No. 5 - Collectors & Collecting
No. 6 - Early Cricket Reporters
No. 7 – Northamptonshire
No. 8 - Cricket & Authors

———————

Details of all James Philip's published books
and forthcoming publications can be found on his
website www.jamesphilip.co.uk

———————

Cover artwork concepts by James Philip
Graphic Design by Beastleigh Web Design

Printed in Great Britain
by Amazon

51678912R00097